*For the friends who shaped my life:
Michael Madonia, Michael Nemeth, Todd Johnson,
Ronald Schultz, Ed Kellett, and Heather Averill Farley*

Acknowledgments

First and foremost, all praise to my brilliant editor, Susan Van Metre, whose hard work and guidance can be found on every page of this book. Also, much thanks to the entire team at Amulet Books, most notably Andrea Colvin and Jason Wells. My thanks also go out to my agent, Alison Fargis, and everyone at The Stonesong Press; Joe Deasy for his insight and humor; my wife, Alison, for her love and inspiration; my mom and dad; Paul Fargis, Molly Choi, Maureen Falvey, Beth Fargis Lancaster, Doug Lancaster, and of course, Daisy.

THE SISTERS GRIMM

THE UNUSUAL SUSPECTS

SABRINA SCRAMBLED THROUGH THE DARKNESS *armed with a shovel and using the cold, stone walls as a guide. Each step was a challenge to her balance and senses. She stumbled over jagged rocks and accidentally kicked over an abandoned tool, sending a clanging echo off the tunnel walls. Whatever was waiting for her in the labyrinth knew she was coming now. Unfortunately, she couldn't turn back. Her family was somewhere in the twisting maze and no one else could help them. Sabrina prayed they were still alive.*

The tunnel made a sharp turn, and around the corner Sabrina spotted a distant, flickering light. She quickened her pace, and soon the tunnel opened into an enormous cave, carved out of the bedrock of Ferryport Landing. Torches mounted on the cave walls gave the room a dull light, not strong enough to dissolve the black shadows in every corner.

Sabrina scanned the cave. A few old buckets and a couple of shovels leaned against a crumbling wall. She started to retrace her steps when something hit her squarely in the back. She fell hard on her shoulder, dropping her shovel. Searing pain swam through her veins, followed by a throbbing ache. She could still move her fingers, but Sabrina knew her arm was broken. She screamed, but her cries were drowned out by an odd clicking and hissing sound.

As she crawled to her feet, Sabrina grabbed the shovel and swung it around threateningly, searching the room for her attacker.

"I've come for my family," she shouted into the darkness. Her voice bounced back at her from all sides of the rocky room.

Again, she heard clicking and hissing, followed by a cold, arrogant chuckle. A long, spindly leg struck out from the shadows, narrowly missing Sabrina's head. It slammed against the wall behind the girl, pulverizing stone into dust. Sabrina lifted the heavy shovel and swung wildly at the leg, sinking the sharp edge deep into the monster's flesh. Shrieks of agony echoed through the cavern.

"I'm not going to be easy to kill," Sabrina said, hoping her voice sounded more confident to the monster than it did to her own ears.

"Kill you? This is a party!" a voice replied. "And you're the guest of honor."

PRAISE FOR THE *SISTERS GRIMM* SERIES:

New York Times Bestseller
Oppenheim Toy Portfolio Platinum Award
Kirkus Best Fantasy Book
A *Real Simple* magazine "Must-Have"

"Mystery meets fairy tale." —The CBS *Early Show*

"Enormously entertaining . . . takes the fractured fairy-tale
genre to new heights." —*Time Out New York Kids*

"Adventure, laughs, and surprises kept me eagerly turning the
pages." —R. L. Stine, author of the *Goosebumps* series

"Kids will love Sabrina and Daphne's adventures as
much as I did." —Sarah Michelle Gellar
(Buffy on *Buffy the Vampire Slayer*)

★ "Features both a pair of memorable young sleuths and a mad-
cap plot." —*Kirkus Reviews,* starred review

"Readers will have trouble putting this novel down."
—*The Dallas Morning News*

ALSO BY MICHAEL BUCKLEY:

In the *Sisters Grimm* series:

BOOK ONE: THE FAIRY-TALE DETECTIVES

BOOK TWO: THE UNUSUAL SUSPECTS

BOOK THREE: THE PROBLEM CHILD

BOOK FOUR: ONCE UPON A CRIME

BOOK FIVE: MAGIC AND OTHER MISDEMEANORS

BOOK SIX: TALES FROM THE HOOD

BOOK SEVEN: THE EVERAFTER WAR

BOOK EIGHT: THE INSIDE STORY

BOOK NINE: THE COUNCIL OF MIRRORS

A VERY GRIMM GUIDE

In the *NERDS* series:

BOOK ONE: NATIONAL ESPIONAGE, RESCUE, AND DEFENSE SOCIETY

BOOK TWO: M IS FOR MAMA'S BOY

BOOK THREE: THE CHEERLEADERS OF DOOM

BOOK FOUR: THE VILLAIN VIRUS

BOOK FIVE: ATTACK OF THE BULLIES

THE SISTERS GRIMM

· BOOK TWO ·

THE UNUSUAL SUSPECTS

MICHAEL BUCKLEY

PICTURES BY PETER FERGUSON

AMULET BOOKS

New York

Library of Congress Cataloging-in-Publication Data:
Buckley, Michael.
The sisters Grimm, book two : the unusual suspects / Michael Buckley ;
illustrated by Peter Ferguson.
p. cm.
Summary: Although filled with anger over her parents' disappearance,
eleven-year-old Sabrina Grimm—along with her grandmother, sister, and
several fairy-tale characters—tries to discover who has killed her teacher.
ISBN 978-0-8109-1610-X
[1. Characters in literature—Fiction. 2. Anger—Fiction. 3.
Sisters—Fiction. 4. Grandmothers—Fiction. 5. Schools—Fiction. 6.
Mystery and detective stories.] I. Title: Unusual suspects. II.
Ferguson, Peter, 1968- ill. III. Title.
PZ7.B882323Siu 2006
[Fic]—dc22
2005024149

Paperback ISBN 978-0-8109-9323-5

Printed and bound in U.S.A.
22 21 20 19 18 17 16 15

Amulet Books are available at special discounts when purchased in quantity for premiums and promotions as well as fundraising or educational use. Special editions can also be created to specification. For details, contact specialsales@abramsbooks.com or the address below.

THE ART OF BOOKS SINCE 1949
115 West 18th Street
New York, NY 10011
www.abramsbooks.com

1

THREE DAYS EARLIER

et's get this party started, already!" Sabrina complained under her breath as she rubbed the charley horse in her leg. She and her seven-year-old sister, Daphne, had been crouching behind a stack of Diaper Rash Donna dolls for nearly three hours. She was tired, hungry, and more than a little irritated. For a week they had been on this "stakeout" and it was beginning to look as if they had wasted another perfectly good night of sleep. Even Elvis, their two-hundred-pound Great Dane, had given up and was snoring on the floor next to them.

Of course, how Sabrina wanted to spend her time wasn't really considered, she had learned, especially if there was a mystery afoot. Their grandmother loved a good mystery, so when Gepetto complained that his toy store had been robbed every night for two weeks, Granny Relda volunteered herself and the sisters

Grimm to help the police catch the crooks. Sabrina wondered what an old woman, two kids, and a sleepy dog could do that the expensive security cameras and motion detectors the old man had installed couldn't, but once Granny sunk her teeth into something she wouldn't let go.

In most towns, the police do not rely on an old woman, two kids, and a sleepy dog to solve crimes, but Ferryport Landing was no ordinary town. More than half of its residents were part of a secret community known as the Everafters. Everafters were actually fairy-tale characters who had fled Europe to escape persecution. Settling in the little river town almost two hundred years ago, they now used magical disguises to live and work alongside their normal neighbors. Ogres worked at the post office, witches ran the twenty-four-hour diner, and the town mayor was the legendary Prince Charming. The humans were none the wiser—except the Grimms.

As fantastic and thrilling as it sounded to live among fairy-tale characters, it wasn't a dream come true for Sabrina Grimm. Being the last in a long line of Grimms (descended from the famous Brothers Grimm), she and her sister had had the family responsibility of keeping the peace between Everafters and humans thrust upon them no less than three weeks ago.

And it wasn't an easy job. Most Everafters saw the Grimms as the bane of their existence. A two-century-old magical curse had trapped the Everafters in Ferryport Landing for all eternity, and the girls' great-great-great-great grandfather Wilhelm was responsible. Trying to prevent a war between Everafters and humans, Wilhelm had aligned himself with a powerful witch named Baba Yaga and together they had cast the spell over the town. The Everafters' freedom could only be returned to them when the last Grimm had passed away, and so far, the Grimms were alive and kicking. Yet even with that kind of baggage, Granny Relda had made a few genuine friends in the community. Sheriff Hamstead was one of those friends. The rotund policeman with the Southern charm was actually one of the three *not-so-little* pigs. Lately, he had turned to the family for help with Ferryport Landing's unsolved cases.

And here the Grimms were, leg cramps and all, waiting for someone or something to make its move. After five long nights, Sabrina's patience had worn thin. There were things she should have been doing, important things, that didn't involve hiding behind Etch-A-Sketches and cans of Silly String stacked miles high for the Christmas season. Sabrina reached into her pocket and pulled out a small flashlight. She flicked its switch and a tiny focused beam illuminated a book sitting at her feet. She picked it up and started reading. She didn't get far.

"Sabrina," Daphne whispered. "What are you doing? You're going to give us away. Turn off that light."

Sabrina grumbled, slammed the book closed, and set it aside. If *The Jungle Book* held any clue to rescuing their parents it would have to wait. Sabrina's little sister had taken to detective work the way a dog does to a slice of bologna. Like their grandmother, Daphne loved every minute of it—the stakeouts, the long hours. She was a natural and took her new job quite seriously.

Suddenly, there was a rustling sound across the room. Sabrina quickly shut off her flashlight and peered over the stack of dolls. Something was moving near a display for a hot holiday toy, Don't Tickle the Tiger. Daphne poked her head up and looked around, too. "Do you see anything?" the little girl whispered.

"No, but it's coming from that direction," Sabrina whispered back. "Wake up Sleepy and see if he smells anything."

Daphne shook Elvis until he staggered to his feet. The big dog had recently had bandages removed after a run-in with a bad guy's boot, and was still a bit sluggish. He looked around as if he didn't remember where he was.

"You smell any bad guys, Elvis?" Daphne asked.

The dog sniffed the air. His ears rose and his eyes grew wide. He let out a soft whine to let the girls know he *had* smelled something.

"Go get 'em, boy!" Daphne cried, and the big dog took off like a rocket.

Unfortunately, that was when Sabrina realized that Elvis's leash had wrapped itself around her foot. As the dog howled wildly and tore through the store, the girl was dragged behind him, knocking over stacks of board games and sending balls bouncing in all directions. They emptied boxes of puzzle pieces and sent an army of Slinkys slinking across the floor. Sabrina struggled to grab the leash, but every time she got close to freeing herself, the dog took a wild turn and sent her skidding.

"Turn on the lights!" Daphne shouted.

"Hey, let me go!" a voice cried out.

"What's the big idea?" another one shouted.

Elvis circled back around, and Sabrina slid into a pile of what felt like sticky leaves. Some clung to her arms and legs and one glued itself to her forehead.

When the lights finally came on, Elvis stopped, stood over Sabrina, and barked. The girl sat up and then looked down at herself. There she was, in the center of Gepetto's Toy Store, covered in sticky glue mousetraps, each of which had a tiny little man, no more than a couple of inches high, stuck quick in the glue.

"Lilliputians," Sabrina said.

"I knew it!" Granny Relda said, appearing from around a stack

of action figures. The old woman, dressed in a bright blue dress and a matching hat with a sunflower appliqué sewn into it, had the nerve to laugh. When Sabrina scowled at her, she tried to stop, but couldn't.

"Oh *liebling*," she giggled in her German accent.

Daphne rushed over and tried to pull one of the traps off of Sabrina's shirt but found it was stuck tight to her sister, as were a dozen or so Lilliputians.

"Who is the sick psychopath that came up with this idea?" one of the Lilliputians shouted indignantly.

Granny leaned down to him and smiled. "Don't worry, a little vegetable oil and we'll have you free in no time."

"But I'm afraid you're under arrest," Sheriff Hamstead said as he stepped out from behind a stack of footballs. His puffy, pink face beamed proudly as he tugged his trousers up over his massive belly. The sheriff was always fighting his sinking slacks.

The Lilliputians groaned and complained as the sheriff went to work yanking the sticky traps off Sabrina's clothes.

"You have the right to remain silent," Hamstead said. "Anything you say can and will be used against you in a court of law."

"Ouch!" said Sabrina as the sheriff tugged the glue-trap from her forehead.

"I'm not talking, copper," one of the Lilliputians snapped. "I'll let my lawyer do the talking when we sue you for police brutality."

"*Police brutality!*" Sheriff Hamstead exclaimed. Unfortunately, when the portly policeman got angry or excited, the magical disguise he used to hide who he really was stopped working. Now his nose vanished and was replaced by a runny, pink snout. Two hairy pig ears popped out of the top of his head and a series of snorts, squeals, and huffs came out of his mouth. Hamstead had nearly completed the change when the security guard from the next store over wandered in.

"What's going on in here?" the guard said with a tough, authoritative voice. He was a tall, husky man with a military-style hair cut. He puffed up his chest and pulled a billy club from a loop on his belt. He eyed the crowd as if he were fully prepared to deal with a gang of crooks, but when he saw the pig in a police uniform hovering over a dozen tiny men in glue traps, his confidence disappeared and his club fell to the floor.

"We forgot some of the shops have their own security guards," Granny Relda said softly as she reached into her handbag and approached the stunned man. She blew some soft pink dust into his face and his eyes glazed over. She told him he'd had another usual night at work and nothing out of the ordinary had occurred. The security guard nodded in agreement.

"Another night at work," he mumbled, falling under the forgetful dust's magic.

Sabrina scowled. She hated when magic was used to fix problems, especially when the problem involved humans.

• • •

"The glue traps were a brilliant idea," Sheriff Hamstead said as he drove the family home in his squad car. Granny sat in the front, enjoying his praise while Sabrina and Daphne were in the back, jockeying with Elvis for seat space. Hamstead had locked the Lilliputians in the glove compartment and whenever their complaining got too loud, he would smack the top of the dashboard with his puffy hand and yell, "Pipe down!"

"I'm just glad we could be of some help," Granny Relda replied. "Gepetto is such a nice old man. It broke my heart to hear he was being robbed, and with Christmas only two weeks away."

"I know the holidays are hard on him; he misses his boy," Hamstead said. "It's hard to believe that in two hundred years no one has heard a peep from Pinocchio."

"Wilhelm's journals claim he refused to get on the boat," Granny replied. "I suppose if I had been swallowed by a shark I wouldn't be too eager to go back to sea either."

"I thought it was a whale," Daphne said.

"No, hon, only in the movie," Granny replied. "It's just a

shame he didn't tell his father. By the time Gepetto discovered he wasn't on board, they were too far out to turn back."

"Well, I really do appreciate your help with this," the sheriff said. "The mayor's been cutting budgets left and right these days and I just didn't have the man power or money to catch the little thieves myself."

"Or make sure that the security guard was off duty so we didn't have to mess with his brain," Sabrina grumbled.

"Sheriff, the Grimms are always at your disposal," Granny Relda said, ignoring Sabrina.

"I appreciate that, Relda, and I wish I could give you the credit for the arrest, but if Mayor Charming found out we'd been working together, my backside would be one of those footballs in Gepetto's store," Hamstead said.

"It's our little secret," Granny Relda said with a wink.

"How is Canis?"

Granny shifted uncomfortably in her seat. Both Sabrina and Daphne watched her closely, wondering what their grandmother would say.

"He's doing just fine," the old woman replied, forcing a smile.

Sabrina couldn't believe what she had just heard. In the short time they had known the old woman, Granny Relda had never told a lie. Mr. Canis was not "fine" by a long shot. Three weeks earlier, Granny's constant companion and houseguest, Mr. Canis, had transformed into the savage creature known as the Big Bad Wolf. Since then, no one had seen him. He had locked himself inside his bedroom while he fought to put back his real-life inner demon. Every night, Sabrina and Daphne had heard the old man's painful moans and labored breathing. They would be woken by one of his horrible cries or the sound of him slamming against a wall. Mr. Canis was far from "fine."

"That's good to hear," Hamstead said, though even from the backseat Sabrina could spot the look of doubt on his face.

"I want my phone call," a little voice cried from the glove compartment. "We were framed!"

The sheriff banged heavily on the dashboard. "Tell it to the judge!"

Soon, Sheriff Hamstead pulled his squad car into the driveway of the family's quaint, two-story yellow house. It was very late and all the lights were off. Sabrina opened her door and Elvis lumbered out, still wearing two Lilliputian-free glue traps on his giant behind. It was bitterly cold, and Sabrina hoped the two adults wouldn't blabber on. Granny could talk a person's ear off. But the sheriff just thanked them again and excused himself, claiming he had paperwork piling up back at the station.

At the front door, Granny took a giant key ring out of her

handbag and went to work unlocking the many locks. Once Sabrina had believed Granny Relda was just a paranoid shut-in, but in the last three weeks she had seen things that she would never have dreamed possible and now understood why the house was locked so tightly.

Granny Relda knocked on the door three times and announced to the house that the family was home, making the last magical lock slide back and the door swing open.

After cookies, and some vegetable-oil swabbing for Elvis, Granny Relda said, "Get cleaned up and hurry to bed. You've got school tomorrow. I've kept you up too late as it is."

"Actually, Granny," Sabrina replied. "I think I'm coming down with something. I'd hate to go to school and get everyone sick."

Granny grinned. "Sabrina, it's been three weeks. If you two don't go to school tomorrow they are going to put me in the jailhouse. Now, up to bed."

Sabrina frowned, forced a cough to make the old woman feel guilty, and then marched up the steps. Couldn't Granny see there were more important things to do than go to school?

• • •

Long after Daphne had drifted into a steady, snoring sleep, Sabrina crawled out of their four-poster bed in the room that had once been their father's. His model airplanes still hung from the ceiling and an old catcher's mitt rested on his desk. She knelt down on her hands and knees and pulled several dusty books and a key ring out from under the bed before climbing to her feet again and creeping silently into the hallway.

Sabrina was very good at creeping. In fact, she'd have said she was an expert. A year and a half in and out of an orphanage and foster homes had taught her how to step lightly on hardwood floors and avoid creaky beams. In the past she had used these skills to escape from one bad situation after another. In eighteen months, the sisters Grimm had run away from more than a dozen foster families. Some of the families had used them as personal servants while others expected them to be punching bags for their own obnoxious children. These days the girls didn't want to run away. Granny Relda had given them a home. But being sneaky still had its advantages. Especially when Sabrina was doing something she knew her grandmother would disapprove of.

When Sabrina reached the door at the top of the steps, she sorted through her own growing collection of keys and found the long brass skeleton key that fit it. Once it was unlocked, she took a quick look around to make sure no one was watching, and then stepped inside.

The room was empty except for a full-length mirror that hung on the far wall. A single window allowed enough moonlight into the room for Sabrina to see by. She stepped up to the mirror and her reflection appeared. Her long blond hair and blue eyes glowed a ghostly milky blue, but Sabrina wasn't here to admire herself. Instead, she did what most people would think was impossible—she walked directly into the glass and disappeared.

The mirror was actually a doorway that led to an immense room Sabrina knew as the Hall of Wonders. In many ways it reminded Sabrina of Grand Central Station in New York City with its incredibly long, barrel-vaulted ceiling supported by towering marble columns. There were literally thousands of arched doorways on either side of the hall. Each door was labeled with a little brass plaque that revealed what was behind it: talking plants; giant living chess pieces; Babe, the Blue Ox; and thousands more impossibly interesting magical items and creatures, all collected by the Grimms for safekeeping. Granny called it the world's biggest walk-in closet. Sabrina had started to see it as her only hope.

She scanned the hall and spotted a lonely figure sitting in a high-backed chair several yards away. She headed in his direction.

"Mirror," the girl said to the short, squat man. "I think I've found something useful."

Mirror, as he was called, was a balding man with deep angular features and thick, full lips who lived inside the mirror. His was the face that had proclaimed Snow White "the fairest one of all" to the Wicked Queen. When he spotted Sabrina, he set a celebrity magazine he had been reading down and got up from his chair.

"I thought you'd given this up," he said.

"Granny's had us pretty busy," Sabrina explained. "So, let's get started."

"What? No *hello*? No *how are you*? *How's the family*?" the little man complained.

"Sorry, Mirror, I don't have a lot of time."

"Apology accepted. So, kiddo, what's on the agenda tonight?"

"I found this thing in Burton's translation of *The Arabian Nights*," Sabrina said, opening one of her books and handing it to Mirror. He didn't even bother to look at the page.

"Listen, blondie, I assure you, if we had a jinni's lamp I'd have a lot more hair on my head and we'd all be living in Hawaii. Sweet-ums, don't you think that if your grandmother had access to that kind of power, your parents would have already been found?"

Sabrina frowned. She would spend the whole day researching ways to rescue her parents from their kidnappers, and every night, Mirror would shoot her ideas down one by one.

"Fine," Sabrina replied, handing Mirror another book she had opened already. "What about this?"

Mirror looked down at the book, flipped it to view its cover, and smiled. "L. Frank Baum, huh? Follow me, little cowpoke. I think we might just have that one in stock."

The little man spun around and headed down the long hallway. "The Golden Cap is one of the most interesting things the Wicked Witch ever owned, yet most people are more fascinated by her broomstick," he continued.

"I've been reading as much as I can," Sabrina replied, doing her best to keep up with Mirror's quick pace.

"Oh, I have no doubt about that," the little man said, spinning around on the girl. "So, you know how it works?"

"Yes, I put it on and the monkeys come. They'll do whatever I want them to."

"The only downside is the monkey smell," Mirror said. "That's a stink that never quite goes away."

After a short hike, Mirror stopped at a door labeled MAGICAL HATS and reached out his hand. Sabrina handed him her key ring.

"You're building quite a collection," he said disapprovingly. "Does your grandmother know you've been swiping her keys and making copies?"

Sabrina shook her head no.

"Well, you've got one for this door," he said. He opened the door and went inside. As Sabrina waited in the hall, she could see him rummaging through the room. He made quite a racket moving things around, knocking over a helmet in the process, which rolled across the floor with a clatter. Soon he returned with a gold-colored hard hat, which held a can of soda on each side. Tubes ran out of the cans and dangled below the chin strap. On the front of the hat the words EMERALD CITY GREEN SOX were printed in big green letters. Mirror dusted it off and handed it to Sabrina.

"This is the Golden Cap the Wicked Witch of the West used to summon the flying monkeys?" she said in disbelief.

"The Witch was a huge sports fan," Mirror replied. "The magic instructions are inside."

"You've got to be kidding me," Sabrina said as she read them.

"Afraid not."

The girl scowled and put the hat on her head. Following the ridiculous instructions, she lifted her right leg and began the crazy spell. *"Ep-pe, pep-pe, kak-ke."*

Mirror turned away and snickered.

"Don't laugh, I feel stupid enough," Sabrina said, lowering her leg and lifting the other. *"Hil-lo, hol-lo, hel-lo."*

"I wish I had a camera." The little man giggled.

"Ziz-zy, zuz-zy, zik!" the girl said, now standing on both feet. Suddenly, her ears filled with the sound of a hundred flapping

wings. Monkeys materialized out of thin air. They gathered around their summoner, grinning and beating their black wings. Sabrina understood immediately why Mirror had warned her about the monkey smell. They were a ripe bunch. She thought she might gag when one of the monkeys, wearing a beanie with a bright blue ball on top, took her hand and gave it a sloppy kiss.

"What is your bidding, master?" it asked in a deep, unearthly voice. Sabrina hadn't gotten used to talking animals yet. They made her nervous.

"OK, uh, Mr. Monkey . . . uh, I need you to go fetch my parents," she commanded.

The monkeys screamed and clapped their hands as if she had just promised them bananas. Their wings started to flap and they leaped into the air. But instead of disappearing as Sabrina expected, they zipped around the hall, flying in all directions, as if they weren't sure which way to go. The leader floated back down to the girl. He had a confused expression on his face.

"What's wrong?" Sabrina asked.

"Great magic blocks our path. Your wish cannot be granted," he said, and as quickly as he and the others had appeared, they were gone.

"Why not?" Sabrina shouted, angrily. She took the obnoxious magic hat off her head and shook it, but the monkeys did not return.

Mirror gave her a sad, pitying smile but Sabrina couldn't bear to look at it. She was exhausted and angry and not a single step closer to finding her parents. How many more dead ends could she come up against?

She forced a smile and handed the Golden Cap back to Mirror. The little man nodded and put it inside its room, shutting the door and locking it behind him.

"Thanks, anyway." She sighed as she took her key ring and silently walked away. She stepped through the portal without looking back and found herself alone again, in the empty room. Crossing the floor, Sabrina suddenly stopped, turned, and looked at herself in the mirror's reflection.

"Mirror?" she called out, softly. A blue mist filled the glass and the little man's squat, muscular head peered out at her.

"Want to take a look?" he asked.

Sabrina nodded.

He winked. "You know how it works."

"Mirror, mirror, near and far, show me where my parents are," the girl said. Once again, the mirror's surface changed. As the little man's face disappeared, Sabrina's parents, Henry and Veronica Grimm, appeared instead. They were lying on a bed in the dark, fast asleep.

Sabrina looked at her parents' faces and sighed. Her father had a round, warm face like her sister's, framed with blond hair. Her mother, Veronica, was beautiful, with high cheekbones and jet-black locks. They looked vulnerable lying there surrounded by darkness.

"I won't let another Christmas go by without you. I'll find a way to bring you home," Sabrina said as she reached out to touch them. Her hand dipped into the magic mirror's reflective surface and her parents' image rippled the way a pond does when a stone is thrown into it. Sabrina stared at them until they faded away.

"Same time tomorrow night?" Mirror said as his face reappeared.

"See you then," Sabrina said, wiping the tears from her cheeks and flashing Mirror a hopeful smile. The little man nodded and his face faded away.

The girl tiptoed back down the hallway, but just as she reached her bedroom she heard a painful groan coming from the room opposite. Mr. Canis was having another difficult night. Sabrina stood in the hallway listening to his painful breathing. She imagined that at any moment the door might explode and the Big Bad Wolf would catch her up in his jaws. What would they do if the Wolf beat Mr. Canis and got loose? What if the old man wasn't strong enough to keep him inside?

But Mr. Canis wasn't the only Everafter she had doubts about lately. The charm of living in a community where fairy godmothers and cowardly lions were her neighbors had worn off and Sabrina was beginning to view the Everafters with suspicion. After all, one of them was responsible for kidnapping her parents. She had decided to keep an eye on them all until her parents were home—Mr. Canis included.

"Go to bed, child," a voice growled. "Or are you going to huff and puff and blow the door in?" The voice startled Sabrina—it sounded like a combination of Canis and the Wolf—and she quickly darted into her bedroom and closed her door tightly. Leaning against it, she realized how dumb she had been. Of course he could smell her through his bedroom door.

2

There were three things that Sabrina took great pride in: one, she had successfully arm wrestled every boy at the orphanage (including two extremely humiliated janitors); two, she wasn't afraid of heights; and three, she wasn't a sissy. But when one wakes up to find a giant hairy spider crawling on one's face, one should be allowed to throw a hissy fit. Which was exactly what Sabrina did.

And her bloodcurdling scream caused Daphne to wake up, see the spider, and scream, too. Daphne's scream just made the whole thing that much more horrible for Sabrina, so she screamed even louder, which caused the little girl to scream at her sister's scream, resulting in a mini-concert of hysteria that went on and on for about five minutes.

Granny Relda burst into their bedroom with Elvis at her side.

Granny's gray hair, still streaked with its former red, was rolled up in huge curlers and tucked underneath a sleeping cap. She wore a bright blue nightgown patterned with little cows jumping over little moons and her face was covered in a mossy-green mud mask that she swore kept her looking young. But her mud mask was not nearly as startling as the deadly sharp broadsword she held in her hand and the fierce battle cry that bellowed from her throat.

Scanning the room for attackers, the old woman said, "My goodness, *lieblings*—what is the matter?"

"That!" Sabrina and Daphne shouted in unison, pointing at a black tarantula the size of a baked potato that had leaped off the bed and now clung to a nearby curtain. Its eight long, hairy legs and vicious-looking pinchers clicked and snapped as it climbed up the drapes.

"Oh, children, it's just a spider," Granny Relda said as she crossed the room and picked the creepy-crawly thing up with her bare hands. Daphne squealed as if she had been the one to touch it and crawled under her blanket to hide.

"Just a spider?" Sabrina cried. "You could put a saddle on that thing!"

"He's South American I believe," Granny said, petting the spider like it was a kitten. "You're a long way from home, friend. How did you find your way here?"

"Like you have to ask!" Sabrina cried.

"Now, now," the old woman said. "It's just a harmless spider."

Elvis trotted over and sniffed the creature. The tarantula raised up two legs and hissed at the Great Dane, causing the usually fearless hound to leap back and yelp in surprise.

"Is it gone yet?" Daphne's muffled voice came from under the covers. "Has it been squished?"

"Girls, Puck's just being a boy. Brothers do these kinds of thing to their sisters all the time," Granny said soothingly.

"He's not our brother!" Sabrina shouted as she crawled out of bed and stomped across the room toward the door.

"Where are you going?" Granny Relda asked.

"To tell Puck's face what my fist thinks of him," the girl said, marching past the old woman and out the door.

"Don't leave me in here with the spider!" Daphne begged, but her sister ignored her plea. Puck was long overdue for a sock in the nose and Sabrina was just the person to give it to him.

Puck, like Mr. Canis, was an Everafter, a four-thousand-year-old fairy in the body of an eleven-year-old boy. Rude, selfish, smelly, and obnoxious, the boy had been taunting Sabrina since he had met her. He'd dumped a bucket of paint on her, rubbed her toothbrush in red-pepper seeds, filled her pockets with bloodworms, and put something in her shoes that still made her shudder when she recalled its smell. Puck also had a slew of magical pranks. He could shape-shift into any animal and several inanimate objects. Sabrina couldn't count how many times he had morphed into a chair and then pulled himself out from under her when she sat down. Why Granny Relda had taken to him was beyond comprehension, especially with his well-documented history. Everyone from William Shakespeare to Rudyard Kipling had warned about Puck's exploits, yet Granny treated him as if he were one of the family and had even invited him to live with the Grimms. Now Sabrina was determined to make the "Trickster King" wish he had declined the invitation.

She marched down the hall to his bedroom. No one had been in Puck's room since it had been built. Glinda the Good Witch and the Three Little Pigs used nails, hammers, and magic to create it and when it was finished, the rude boy hadn't bothered to invite anyone in to see the final result. So, when Sabrina opened the door and stepped inside, she was amazed by what she found. Puck's room was impossible.

There were trees and grass and a stone path and a waterfall that spilled into a lagoon. There was an actual sky with clouds and kites where the ceiling should have been. In the center of a clearing was a wrestling ring in which a kangaroo wearing boxing gloves and shorts sat lazily waiting for his next challenger. A roller coaster sailed on a track above Sabrina and an ice-cream truck sat off to one side. In the center of it all was Puck, perched on an enormous throne, wearing his stupid golden crown. He was eating an ice-cream cone that held half a dozen different flavored scoops, all of which were dripping down his arm.

Poor Sabrina was so astonished by her surroundings that she failed to notice the metal plate at her feet. When she stepped onto it, she triggered the release of an egg, which rolled down a narrow track and fell onto a rusty nail that cracked its shell in half. The egg then emptied its drippings onto a skillet, which triggered the striking of a match that ignited a gas burner. Soon, the egg was popping and crackling as the heat from the flame cooked it, causing steam to rise, which, in turn, filled a balloon that rose into the air. The balloon was connected by a string to a small lever that tipped a bucket of water into a drinking glass sitting on the high end of a seesaw. The seesaw tilted downward from the weight, untying a rope that held a heavy sandbag. The sandbag fell to the ground and hit a bright red button and then it all came to a stop.

And, unfortunately, that's when Sabrina noticed the bizarre contraption.

"What the—?" she said aloud but just then a buzzer drowned out her voice and the girl was catapulted off the metal plate and up, up through the air and then down, down into a large vat of goo, causing an enormous splash.

"Doesn't anyone knock around here?" Puck complained when Sabrina finally fought her way to the surface.

"What is this stuff?" she cried, as she struggled through the vat of thick white mush in which several dark chunks floated. The stink of it nearly made Sabrina barf.

"It's a big tub of glue and buttermilk, of course," the boy said, as if it were obvious. "With some bread-and-butter pickles added for flavor. It's quite stinky."

"You're going to pay for this, Puck!" Sabrina screamed as she climbed out of the tub. She wiped her face as well as she could and flared her nostrils.

"There she is, Miss America," the prankster sang. He tossed his huge ice-cream cone into the wrestling ring and the boxing kangaroo lapped it up happily. Then the boy jumped into the air and two massive pink-streaked insect wings sprang from his back. Soon he was soaring high above Sabrina.

"Just like an Everafter to use magic to run from a fight! Come down here, you smelly little freak," Sabrina shouted.

"With our fists?" Puck cried indignantly. "Human, I'm royalty. A prince fights like a prince."

His wings flapped loudly as he flew across his forest room to a nearby table. He scooped up two swords and flew back to Sabrina, tossing one at her feet as he floated effortlessly to the ground.

The girl grabbed her weapon and held it confidently. It was made of wood, like Puck's, but it would still hurt if she got a good whack at him.

The two children circled each other. Sabrina wasted no time thrusting her sword at the boy, who immediately floated several feet off the ground and spun easily, dodging her attack. While she was off balance, Puck flew toward her, trying to strike her arm. But Sabrina shifted her weight, swung her sword, and hit him on the top of his head.

"Dirty little snotface!" the boy cried as he rubbed his sore noggin. "Someone's been learning."

"Charge me again and you'll see what else I've learned, horse-breath!" Sabrina threatened.

Puck flew at her, swinging his wooden sword toward her

shoulder, only to have it blocked by Sabrina's sword. She took a swipe at his belly, missing him by less than an inch.

"*Tsk, tsk*. Looks like you haven't learned the most important lesson of all." He laughed. "Always protect your butt."

Puck spun around and smacked Sabrina on the backside with his sword. The blow felt like the sting of a dozen honeybees, but Sabrina would never give him the satisfaction of hearing her cry out in pain.

"You're as slow as you are ugly," the boy taunted.

"You miserable little stink-pig!" Sabrina screamed, wildly slashing at him. He easily dodged each attack, leaping and flying out of the way, even flipping over her head. When he landed, he jammed his sword into her back and chuckled.

"Too bad, you're dead," he said. "You've got to get a hold of that temper. It beats you every time."

Sabrina tossed her sword down angrily and spun around on him with her fists clenched. Seeing that she meant to knock his head off, Puck did what anybody would do when facing an angry Sabrina Grimm—he ran. She chased him around the lagoon, through some heavy brush, out the other side, and right into Granny Relda. The old woman stood over them, and her expression, or what they could see of it behind her beauty mask, was disapproving.

The mask seemed to make a big impression on Puck.

"Old lady!" he cried—he always called Granny Relda by that name. "Your face! You've been cursed by a hobgoblin!"

"*Lieblings,* that's enough of this nonsense," Granny said as the dirty boy scampered to his feet and hid behind her.

"First of all, in my defense, the chain saw was propped on the door and was only supposed to scare her," he said. "If someone got hurt, it wasn't my fault."

"Puck, we're talking about the spider," Granny Relda said.

"Oh, the spider. How did it go off? Were they scared out of their wits?" he asked. "Which one of them wet the bed?"

"I know you didn't mean any harm," the old woman said. "But the girls do have school today and it would have been nice to have a quiet, chaos-free morning, for once."

Puck looked into her face as if she were speaking another language. "And what would be the fun in that?"

"Let's back up!" Sabrina demanded. "What chain saw?"

Granny ignored the question and took the boy's hand. She placed the tarantula into it and smiled kindly. "Let's put this somewhere safe."

Puck took the spider and rubbed its furry back softly. "It's OK, little guy. Did the big ugly girl scare you? I know, she's gruesome, but you're safe now."

Sabrina growled.

"What's going on in here?" Daphne said from the doorway. The little girl rubbed the sleep out of her eyes and then looked around. "Holy cow!"

"Daphne, move off the plate you're standing on," her sister warned, but the little girl just gawked at Puck's room.

"You've got an ice-cream truck," she cried as the roller coaster whipped along its track above her. "And a roller coaster!"

"Daphne, listen to me," Sabrina shouted, but the egg was already cooking. The balloon was already floating upward.

"Sabrina, why do you look like a booger?" the little girl asked as the seesaw fell. The alarm sounded and, just as it had done to Sabrina, the catapult fired Daphne into the air and sent her flailing into the vat of goo. When she landed, she struggled to stand up and wipe the slime from her face.

"What is this?" she asked.

"Glue and buttermilk!" Puck shouted.

"And bread-and-butter pickles," Sabrina added, picking a squishy slice of pickle from behind her ear and tossing it to the ground.

Daphne's face curled up in confusion as if she couldn't get her brain around the idea. Then a huge smile came to her face.

"I want to do it again!" She laughed.

Granny Relda helped Daphne out of the sticky soup.

"Look at us," Sabrina said. "We can't go to school today!" Suddenly, her anger at Puck faded. *We can't go to school today! I can do more research!* she thought.

"Oh *lieblings*, you've already been out for three weeks. I don't want you to get too far behind," Granny said, eyeing the girls and fighting a smile that eventually won the battle.

"We'll just go tomorrow, then," Sabrina suggested.

Before Granny Relda could respond, Mr. Canis appeared at the door, fully dressed in his oversized suit. He looked exhausted and feverish, even more frail than before his transformation, which was startling. He looked like he could use another three weeks in bed.

"The children have a guest," he said, leaning unsteadily against the doorframe.

"Thank you, Mr. Canis," Granny Relda said sounding quite motherly. "You go and get your rest."

The old man nodded and shuffled back toward his room.

"Who's here to see you?" Puck said enviously.

Sabrina shrugged and turned to follow Granny Relda downstairs, with Daphne and Puck following eagerly. As the family entered the living room they spotted a skinny old woman in a drab business suit standing by a bookshelf. She picked up a book with her bony hand and scrutinized the title. Sabrina knew the book. It was called *Mermaids Are People, Too.* The skinny woman tossed it aside and turned to face them, and before Sabrina saw the woman's face, she knew who it was.

"Good morning, girls," Ms. Smirt said. "Did you miss me?"

3

Minerva Smirt hadn't changed since the last time the girls had seen her. The caseworker was still ugly and tired-looking. Her bones still poked out of her clothes as if they were trying to escape her body, and she still had the same angry scowl on her face that she'd had when she left them on the train platform three weeks before. She gazed over her long hooked nose and studied the family scornfully. Puck cringed when her eyes swept over him.

"My, my, my," she said disapprovingly.

"Ms. Smirt, what a pleasant surprise," Granny Relda said without much conviction. "It's so nice to see you again."

"Girls, get your things," Ms. Smirt said, staring into the old woman's eyes. "You're going back to the orphanage."

Daphne slipped her hand into her sister's and squeezed so hard it hurt.

"What in heavens for?" Granny Relda exclaimed.

"Because, Mrs. Grimm, you've been completely negligent," the caseworker barked.

"What does *negligent* mean?" Daphne asked.

"It means she's a failure," Ms. Smirt said, interrupting Sabrina, who usually answered Daphne's vocabulary questions. "It means she's refused to do what the state requires of her. It means she is unfit!

"You two haven't had a day of school since you arrived," the caseworker continued. "I sent your grandmother a letter reminding her about the *law*, but I never heard back. So I sent another, and then another, and then another. But, still I heard nothing, so because your granny can't find the time to put pen to paper and assure me that you two will be educated, I had to get on a five a.m. train and sit next to man who sniffed his own armpits over and over again, for two hours. Imagine how thrilled I am to find out that not only have you two *not* been in school for a month, you obviously haven't seen a bathtub or a bar of soap, either!"

"Who is this woman?" Puck asked.

"Her name's Minerva Smirt. She was our caseworker from the orphanage," Sabrina answered.

"Cranky old buzzard, isn't she?" the boy replied.

Sabrina smiled. *Puck sure has his moments,* she thought.

"And who are you supposed to be?" Ms. Smirt asked, turning her angry face toward the boy. "The king of snot-nosed delinquents?"

Puck smiled. "Finally, someone who has heard of me!"

"This is my nephew visiting from . . . uh . . . Akron, Ohio," Granny said as she snatched Puck's crown off his head. "Ms. Smirt, I assure you the girls were going to go to school today. We've gotten a little sidetracked with visiting and such."

The truth was that Sabrina and Daphne had made every excuse to avoid school. After the family had foiled a plot by Jack (of the beanstalk story) to release giants into the world so he could kill them and regain his fame, the girls convinced their grandmother they needed some time to recover. Then Sabrina had come down with a *mysterious* stomach flu that Daphne conveniently got the next week. A series of stubbed toes, allergic reactions, dizzy spells, bronchial attacks, and food poisonings had continued to keep them out of the classroom, giving them time to do what they both thought was more important— research. Granny's immense and disorganized library of books on all things magical probably held the key to finding and rescuing the girls' parents, missing now for almost two years. The sisters Grimm were in agreement for once: School could wait until Henry and Veronica Grimm were home.

"You understand, Ms. Smirt," Granny Relda continued. "After all, I haven't seen Sabrina since she was a week old."

"And now you aren't going to see her until she's eighteen," the caseworker said. She grabbed the sisters roughly and pulled them toward the door. "Girls, we've got a train to catch. We'll send for your things."

Just then, Elvis trotted into the room. He spotted Ms. Smirt and his usually happy face instantly turned ferocious. He charged the caseworker, sending her tumbling backward over a pile of books, then stood over her, bearing his teeth and growling.

"Get this thing away from me or we'll be making a stop at the pound, too," Ms. Smirt shouted, waving a book at the dog in a fruitless attempt to intimidate him. Granny Relda stepped forward to help the woman, but Sabrina and Daphne stopped her. Instead, the girls stood on either side of the dog and looked down at their caseworker.

"Call him off!" Ms. Smirt demanded.

"Not until you understand what's going to happen today," Sabrina said. "My sister and I are going to go upstairs and get cleaned up. We're going to get dressed and then you are going to take us to school. Then you are going back to New York City, alone."

"You don't get to make the rules, young lady," Ms. Smirt snapped.

"Then we'll just let you and Elvis work out your problems on your own," Daphne said, patting the big dog on his head. "I guess you could probably make a run for it, but you won't get far. Elvis can smell evil."

Elvis barked viciously.

Ms. Smirt stared at the girls for a long moment and then furrowed her brow. "Go get ready for school," she snarled.

• • •

Despite her delay tactics, Sabrina was actually looking forward to her first day of the sixth grade. School offered her something that Granny Relda's house didn't—normal people. She would be surrounded by dull teachers and glassy-eyed kids, watching the clock tick slowly, and she would be as happy as a pig in mud. When you lived with a flying boy and the Big Bad Wolf, a little boredom was welcome.

Sabrina had even planned how her first day would go. She would melt into the crowd and do her best not to draw any attention to herself. She wouldn't join any clubs or raise her hand, but would drift through the day like an invisible girl. She would find some kids to befriend and they would sit together at lunchtime and maybe pass notes in class. Just like normal kids. It was going to be one long, dull, happy experience.

Unfortunately, Smirt was ruining Sabrina's plan. It's hard to be just another face in the crowd when you're being dragged down the hallway by your ear. Not that it was entirely Ms. Smirt's fault that Sabrina was getting attention. Even after three vigorous washings, the girl's hair was still full of goo from Puck's booby trap. It stuck out in a thousand different directions like a hungry octopus. Daphne, on the other hand, had sculpted her hair into an old-fashioned beehive style that spiraled high on her head. Inside the sticky tower, the little girl had inserted several pencils and pens, a ruler, a protractor, two gummy erasers, and a package of peanut-butter crackers for later. By the time the girls got to the principal's office, Sabrina was sure every kid in the school thought that Ferryport Landing Elementary was now enrolling escaped mental patients.

"Excuse me, I'm Minerva Smirt from the New York City Department of Child Welfare," Ms. Smirt said, pounding impatiently on a bell that sat on the counter of the school office. Two middle-aged secretaries were busy spraying bug spray at something in the far corner of the room. The one with the thick glasses leaned down and smacked whatever it was with a magazine, while the chubby one stomped on it like an Irish folk dancer.

"I think it's dead," the chubby one said as she bent over to get a better look.

Smirt rang the bell again, and the two women looked at her as if she had just come in with a flamethrower.

"I'm in a hurry," the caseworker said. "I need to enroll these two orphans."

"We are not orphans!" Sabrina and Daphne said. Ms. Smirt pinched them each on the shoulder for arguing with her.

The bespectacled secretary crossed the room and snatched the bell away. Once she had tossed it into a drawer, she looked up at the caseworker and frowned.

"I'll see if our guidance counselor, Mr. Sheepshank, is available," she said as she eyed the children in bewilderment. Shaking her head, she stepped over to a door and knocked on it lightly.

"Sir, we have some new students . . . I think," the secretary said, turning back and eyeing the girls' odd hairdos.

"Yes! Yes! Please bring them in," a happy voice called. The secretary ushered the trio into the office and closed the door.

Mr. Sheepshank was a little man dressed in a green suit and a bow tie with smiley faces on it. He had a round, full, friendly face with freckled cheeks as red as his hair. When he smiled, little wrinkle lines formed in the corners of his glittering eyes.

"Good morning, ladies. I'm Casper Sheepshank, your school counselor," the man said cheerily. "Welcome to Ferryport Landing Elementary."

Mr. Sheepshank took Ms. Smirt's hand in his and shook it vigorously. The caseworker blushed; and she did something Sabrina had never seen before: She smiled.

"I'm Minerva . . . Minerva Smirt from the New York City Department of Child Welfare," she said.

"It's a pleasure to meet you," the guidance counselor replied. "And who are these lovely ladies?"

"Introduce yourselves, girls," Ms. Smirt said, giggling.

"I'm Sabrina Grimm," Sabrina said. Sheepshank seized her hand and gave her the same joint-jarring treatment he had given to Ms. Smirt.

"I'm Daphne Grimm," Daphne chirped.

"Grimm? You wouldn't happen to be related to Henry Grimm?" the counselor asked.

"He's our dad," Sabrina said.

"He went to school here with us, too," Mr. Sheepshank said. "I remember him quite clearly. He was always getting into trouble. I assume I can expect more of the same from the two of you?"

Unsure of how to respond, the girls said nothing. After a long, uncomfortable pause Sheepshank chuckled and winked at Sabrina. "Just a joke, ladies. Your father was a model student."

"The girls were in my custody for a year and a half until we placed them here in Ferryport Landing with their grandmother, Relda," Ms. Smirt explained. "Unfortunately, Mrs. Grimm has not taken their educations seriously and they've been out of school for a month."

"Better late than never." The counselor laughed as he pulled some paperwork out of a desk drawer, and began to write.

"Casper," Ms. Smirt said, unbuttoning the top button of her shirt. "I wouldn't be able to sleep at night if I didn't warn you about these two. They are quite a handful. I tried to place them in good homes more than a dozen times, and each time it ended in chaos and grief. Nothing was ever good enough for them. They ran away from one foster home just because they were asked to help around the house."

"It wasn't a house! It was a stable," Sabrina said defensively.

"A pony got into my suitcase and ate all my underpants," Daphne added.

"They're also very argumentative," Ms. Smirt said, reaching under the desk and giving each girl a hard pinch on the leg.

"Well, Ms. Smirt," Mr. Sheepshank said, smiling warmly at

the girls. "Here at Ferryport Landing Elementary we like to set our sights on the future. Our motto is 'Everyone deserves a second chance.'"

"Well, I'll tell you, Casper, as a professional who's worked with children for almost twenty years, I'd say a second chance is the last thing a child needs. What most of them need is a swift kick in the . . ."

"Thanks for the warning, Ms. Smirt," the counselor interrupted.

"Please, call me *Minerva*," the skinny woman purred. "You'll need their transcripts of course. I could bring them up Friday. It's just a two-hour trip. Maybe we could discuss their files over dinner."

There was a long, uncomfortable silence. Mr. Sheepshank blushed and then shuffled some papers on his desk.

"Bring them up? All the way from New York City? That's not necessary. Just drop them in the mail when you get a chance," he said, staring down at his paperwork. "Well, I better get these girls started. I trust you can find your way out, Ms. Smirt?"

The caseworker shifted in her chair and her face turned red with frustration. "Of course," she said. She reached into her handbag and took out a card. "Here's my card if you need any help with them. My home phone is on there, too."

Sabrina gazed down at the caseworker's handbag. When she spotted a book entitled *Finding Mr. Right,* the unsettling truth about what she was witnessing revealed itself. Ms. Smirt was flirting. An image of the two grown-ups kissing burned into Sabrina's permanent memory and she shuddered as if she had just witnessed a car crash.

But what was really bothering Sabrina was the odd feeling forming in her own heart. She felt pity for the cranky old woman. Sabrina might not have had much experience with boys, but it was obvious Mr. Sheepshank wasn't into Ms. Smirt, even though the caseworker kept on trying.

"Well, Susie . . . Debbie, I'm off," the skinny woman said as she got up from her chair.

"Sabrina," Sabrina said. Her sympathy vanished.

"Daphne," Daphne added.

Ms. Smirt stopped and turned at the door. "Maybe we'll talk again, Casper . . ."

Mr. Sheepshank smiled but said nothing. He only stared at her as if he were a deer caught in front of a speeding truck. After several way-too-long, painful moments of silence, Ms. Smirt stepped into the hallway.

"Be good girls," the caseworker said as she closed the door. "Or I'll be back."

"Well, I suppose we should get you two to class," said Mr. Sheepshank as he rose from his desk and led them back into the hallway. "Ladies, the first day of school can be difficult for some students. But I want you to know that if there are any bumps in the road—for example, someone you can't get along with or a teacher who's given you too much homework—then I'm the man to come to. Feel free to stop by my office anytime you want. My job is to listen and my door is always open."

Sabrina liked Sheepshank's attitude. She'd been in a dozen schools in the last two years and no one had ever spoken to her the way their new counselor did. While everyone else lectured about learning responsibility and the value of hard work, he seemed to understand how hard it was to be a kid.

"Mr. Sheepshank!" a man shouted from the other end of the hall. He had a German accent not unlike Granny Relda's. "We are due for a conversation!"

The man rushed toward them. He was a tall, dark-haired man in a gray suit. He had a long, lean, ruddy face that made his crooked nose look enormous. Because he was upset, his big bushy eyebrows bounced around on his forehead like excited caterpillars.

"Children, this is your principal, Mr. Hamelin," the guidance counselor said, ignoring the man's frustration. "Mr. Hamelin,

I'd like to introduce you to our new students, Sabrina and Daphne Grimm."

"My grandmother says hello," Daphne said.

Principal Hamelin cocked an eyebrow, aware now that the girls knew who he really was. Granny Relda had told them there were two Everafters working at Ferryport Landing Elementary: Snow White, who was a teacher, and the principal, aka "The Pied Piper of Hamelin." The girls knew his story. Using his magical bagpipes, Hamelin had enchanted a thousand rats to follow him out of town and into the ocean, where they drowned. Granny had explained that Hamelin had gotten his job based on his leadership skills. If he could lead a bunch of rodents, he could handle a school full of kids.

"Of course, of course," Hamelin said, forcing a smile onto his face. "Welcome to Ferryport Landing Elementary. I needed to discuss the . . . uh . . . textbook shortage with Mr. Sheepshank, but it can wait. I hope you'll help them settle in, Casper?"

"My pleasure, Mr. Hamelin," the counselor replied, leading the girls down the hallway. Soon, they stopped in front of a classroom and Mr. Sheepshank patted Daphne on the shoulder. "This is your class."

The girls peered through the window in the door and saw a woman so stunningly beautiful Sabrina could hardly believe it.

Her jet-black hair and porcelain skin were hypnotic. Her eyes were a dazzling blue and her teeth were so white they were nearly blinding.

"Daphne, your teacher's name is Ms. White," Sheepshank said.

Daphne put the palm of her hand into her mouth and bit on it. It was an odd little habit she had when she was very excited.

"I'm so happy," the little girl said giddily, "I might barf."

Ever since Granny Relda had told them that Snow White was a teacher, Daphne had prayed on hands and knees each night that she would be placed in the legendary beauty's class. It looked as if someone had been listening to the little girl's prayers.

"Don't put any crayons in your nose," Sabrina joked as Mr. Sheepshank led her sister into the room. Daphne stuck her tongue out in reply.

As the guidance counselor introduced Daphne, Sabrina studied the teacher through the open door. Snow White and Mr. Hamelin were both Everafters. Could they be trusted? Suspicion clouded Sabrina's mind and anger flowed over her. Maybe Snow White and the Piper were in on her parents' disappearance. Maybe they were working together to kidnap her and her sister next.

"Sabrina, are you feeling OK?" Mr. Sheepshank asked. The girl hadn't noticed him step back into the hall. She nodded.

"Yes, just got a headache," Sabrina replied. It wasn't a lie. Her head was pounding.

"Check with the school nurse if it doesn't go away," the counselor instructed, as he directed her down the hall and up a flight of stairs. On the second floor was another long hallway full of classrooms. They stopped at the first door and Sheepshank opened it. He turned to Sabrina and gave her a warm smile. "I think this might just be the perfect homeroom for you."

"Mr. Grumpner," he said as he stepped into the classroom. "I'd like to introduce you and the class to a new student. Her name is Sabrina Grimm. She and her sister just moved to Ferryport Landing from New York City."

"She looks like she stuck a fork into a light socket," a boy called from the middle of the room. He was short with wiry black hair and big bug eyes. A few kids snickered, but most of the class seemed to be asleep, or about to doze off.

"Toby, shut up," the teacher growled. The boy's face turned red with rage and he looked as if he might actually get out of his seat and charge at the old man. A pretty girl with platinum blond hair and big green eyes put her hand on the boy's arm and it seemed to calm him down.

Grumpner turned his attention to Sabrina. He was an old man with saggy jowls and thin, charcoal-colored hair. To the girl, he looked like a deflating birthday party balloon you find in the garage a week after the fun is over. He frowned.

"Sit," he said gruffly as he pointed to several empty desks in the last row. Then he turned back to the guidance counselor. "Sheepshank, what is wrong with these kids?" he demanded. "Half of them are asleep and the other half are between naps!"

"I'm sure you'll find a way to get them motivated, Mr. Grumpner," the counselor said, as he waved to Sabrina and left the room. "After all, you're one of our finest teachers."

The compliment did little to calm the old man down.

"Open your books to page one forty-two," Grumpner growled, as he walked down the aisle and tossed a ratty textbook onto Sabrina's desk. She opened it and looked for page 142, but it and dozens more pages had been ripped out.

"You need to read this page carefully, morons," Grumpner threatened. "Tomorrow you're going to have a quiz on it."

Sabrina slowly raised her hand.

"What is it, Grimm?"

"That page has been ripped out of my book," she stuttered.

Grumpner's face turned red. Even from the back of the room, Sabrina could spot a throbbing vein on his forehead, preparing to explode. Luckily, the old grouch was distracted by a short, pudgy boy running into the classroom. He rushed past the teacher and hurried down Sabrina's aisle, where he slipped behind a desk and opened a book.

"Wendell!" Grumpner bellowed at the top of his lungs. The chubby boy looked up from his desk, wiped his nose with a handkerchief, and looked genuinely surprised by the teacher's anger. It took all of Sabrina's willpower not to break out laughing at the boy's dumbfounded expression.

"Yes, Mr. Grumpner," Wendell replied.

"You are late, again," the teacher said.

"I'm sorry. I forgot to set my alarm clock," the boy said meekly.

"You forgot?" Grumpner exploded. "Well, that's just great! I bet you didn't forget breakfast this morning! Everyone can see that! Maybe we should cover your alarm clock with candy and French fries; then you'd never forget to set it!"

"I said I was sorry!"

The old man stomped down the aisle and roughly pulled the boy out of his seat. He dragged him to the front of the room so everyone could see his humiliation.

"Do you know why you are always late, Wendell?" Mr. Grumpner asked. "It's because you are a worthless fat-body. Isn't that right?"

This woke up the class, who roared with laughter. Toby, the bug-eyed boy, nearly fell out of his chair giggling.

"Well, I'm sure I could stand to lose a little weight, but I wouldn't go so far as to say . . . !" but the chubby boy never got to finish. Grumpner shoved a piece of chalk into his hand and spun him toward the chalkboard.

"And you are going to write it until the end of this class. You may think that because you're the principal's son you don't have to play by the rules, but I'm not afraid of your father. I have tenure. Get started!"

Wendell turned to the chalkboard and wrote I AM A WORTH-LESS FAT-BODY. The students roared with laughter again, but Sabrina barely noticed. She was too stunned by what Mr. Grumpner had said. Wendell was the principal's son—the child of an Everafter? Sabrina had never imagined that the Everafters might have children or that they would send them to a school where all the other kids were human. She gazed around the room, watching the rest of the class laugh at the boy as he scrawled the mean sentence over and over again. Could any of them be Everafters, too?

• • •

As Sabrina drifted from class to class, she began to realize that Mr. Grumpner wasn't the only teacher on the verge of a nervous breakdown. In fact, the entire sixth-grade faculty was a collection of bullying, screaming nightmares. They shouted through most of their classes, dishing out detentions like scoops of ice cream. Not that Sabrina could really blame them, though. The kids in her classes were real pains in the butt. They slept through the lectures and none of them had done their homework.

Even in gym class, the kids staggered around exhausted. Unfortunately for them, gym class turned out to be the one place you really needed to be alert. Their teacher was Ms. Spangler. Spangler the Strangler, as the kids called her, was a bulky little woman with a ponytail and an evil glint in her eye, who apparently knew how to teach just one game—dodgeball. Sabrina had played dodgeball many times at school in New York City. She considered herself to be pretty good at it; she remembered being the last kid standing many times, so in Ms. Spangler's class, when the first rubber ball smacked her in the head and made her brains rattle in her skull, she knew that something about this dodgeball game was different.

Getting knocked out of the game early gave Sabrina a chance to study the other kids. It was easy to see who the dangerous ones were—the only two really playing the game. Sabrina recognized one as the giggling idiot Toby, from her homeroom class, but the other was a knuckle-dragging hulk with ratty hair. To be honest, Sabrina wasn't sure if it was a boy or a girl; all she knew was that Toby and It were vicious. Together, they whipped balls at the other kids at alarming speeds. When a kid fell down, the duo would pummel him or her mercilessly with the hard rubber balls. Even worse, Ms. Spangler encouraged the craziness. She ran around the gymnasium blowing her whistle and pointing out the weaknesses of the players to Toby and the big It, urging them to target the pudgy, small, slow, and awkward. Whenever a kid was hit and eliminated, Ms. Spangler clapped happily, like a child on Christmas morning.

There was only one other kid in the class who had the energy to defend herself. Sabrina recognized her, too. The pretty blond from Sabrina's homeroom managed to duck out of the way of several shots, dodging and jumping until she, too, was struck and tossed out of the game. She joined the battered kids waiting on the sidelines. When she spotted Sabrina, she smiled and waved. It was the first act of kindness Sabrina had experienced the whole day.

By lunchtime, Sabrina was bruised and belittled, but her main concern was Daphne. Sabrina could handle a screaming teacher or a bully, but her sister was only seven. This school would eat her alive.

Once Sabrina had her tray of food, she searched the cafeteria for her little sister, fully expecting Daphne to be huddled in a corner bawling her eyes out. She was stunned to find her sitting at a table packed with bright-eyed, happy kids, all hanging on her every word. As Sabrina approached the table, the children exploded with laughter watching her sister pull a ruler out of her big beehive hair.

"Daphne, you are the funniest person I have ever met," one of her little friends said.

"Are you OK?" Sabrina asked her sister.

Daphne smiled and nodded. "Time of my life."

Daphne was the hit of the second grade and Sabrina wasn't about to take it away from her. Instead, she trudged through the cafeteria looking for an empty table. She thought she had found one, but just as she was about to sit down, two kids quickly slipped into the seats as if she weren't there at all. She moved in the direction of another deserted table but the same thing happened again. Sabrina was starting to wonder if she could eat standing up, when she felt her feet come out from under her. Her tray flew forward, sending her lunch splattering across the cafeteria. She slammed to the ground hard, pounding her chin into the cold floor, and saw little lights explode in front of her eyes.

Standing over her was the It from gym class. The kid was ape-like, with long, thick arms, a hulking body, and an under-bite.

When Sabrina spotted the little pink ribbon sticking out of Its knotted hair, she finally realized It was a girl.

"Ooops," the girl grunted. Toby, the bug-eyed weirdo, was standing next to her, laughing.

As embarrassed as she was, Sabrina wasn't at all surprised. She had been bullied before. The orphanage had been like a prison at times, and the new kids always got the worst of it until they proved they could give as well as they got.

"You did that on purpose," she said as she calmly got to her feet.

"What are you going to do about it, Grimm? Cry on me?" the big girl laughed.

"If you know my name, then you should know I don't cry," Sabrina said, clenching her fist tightly and then socking the girl in the face. As the big goon fell backward, Sabrina's dreams of dull school days fell with her. For when she turned to look around the cafeteria, the sleepy-faced kids from her class were now wide awake and in awe of her.

"You shouldn't have done that," Toby hissed.

"You're exactly right," a voice shouted. A meaty hand grabbed Sabrina's arm and dragged her away. It was Mr. Grumpner and the vein on his forehead was throbbing.

"She started it," Sabrina cried.

"And I'm ending it," Grumpner shouted back.

• • •

Sabrina sat in Mr. Sheepshank's hot, windowless office waiting for her punishment. The mousy secretary with the thick glasses told her that the guidance counselor would be with her as soon as he was available. Three hours later, he still hadn't shown up.

Sabrina sat and reflected on her day so far. Apparently, the sixth grade was a nightmare, and no one had been courteous enough to let her know in advance. She thought it would be all books and tests—not guerilla warfare. The kids were hateful. The teachers were despicable. It was just like being back in the orphanage.

By the time Mr. Sheepshank and his smiley-face bow tie showed up, Sabrina was seething with rage. Mr. Grumpner followed him into the office, looking indignant, and the two men sat down.

"So, Sabrina," the counselor said. "Do you want to tell us why Natalie is in the school infirmary with a black eye?"

"I'll tell you why!" Mr. Grumpner growled, nearly jumping out of his seat. "This one is trouble."

Mr. Sheepshank sat back in his chair and licked his lips as if he were preparing for a big meal. "Go on, Sabrina, what happened?"

"That ugly freak tripped me on purpose," Sabrina said, wiping the sweat from her brow.

"That's what *she's* saying," Grumpner interrupted. "I saw the whole thing."

"If you'd seen the whole thing, then we wouldn't be sitting here!" Sabrina snapped, surprised by how quickly her anger had boiled over. Her head was starting to pound again. Maybe she was getting sick.

"Listen to that attitude," her teacher bellowed. "I don't know how school works in the big city, but in my classroom you will respect me or else!"

"Yeah, I've seen what 'or else' means in your classroom," the girl said. "I've seen how you teach children to respect you. You insult them, make fun of them, and drag them around. I dare you to try it on me! I just dare you!"

Mr. Grumpner backed away as if he had just stumbled upon a hornet's nest. "Are you going to let her talk to me like that?" he whined to the counselor.

"I believe that letting your feelings out is healthy," Mr. Sheepshank said. "Sabrina has a right to defend herself."

"Save your new-age psychobabble," the teacher grumbled. "What are you going to do to punish her?"

"Punish me?" Sabrina cried. "I didn't start the fight!"

"Mr. Grumpner, I think we need a breather," the counselor

said as he rose from his chair. He crossed the room, took the grouchy teacher by the arm, and led him to the door. "If you spot any more slug-fests, please be sure to bring them to my attention immediately."

"You didn't tell me what you're going to do with her," Grumpner argued, but Mr. Sheepshank just pushed him out of the room and closed the door in his face. "Discipline is the backbone of education!" the teacher shouted through the door. "We'll see what Principal Hamelin thinks about this!"

The guidance counselor ignored the teacher's threat and returned to his chair with a broad smile. "Interesting first day you are having," he said.

"I didn't start that fight but I'm not going to let someone pick on me, either," Sabrina said.

"I'm not asking you to," Sheepshank replied. "I think Natalie got what she had coming to her. She's been pushing kids around since kindergarten. I bet it felt pretty good to knock her down."

Sabrina was stunned. Adults always said you should try to talk out your problems first. "Aren't you supposed to tell me that fighting isn't the answer?" she asked.

"Let's just pretend I did," Mr. Sheepshank continued with a wink. "Sabrina, I know being in the sixth grade isn't easy. There are lots of things that aren't fair, like a bully picking on you. It's a natural human emotion to get angry. So what are you supposed to do? Bottle it up? Well, we all know what happens when you shake up a bottle of soda. It explodes all over the place when you open it. I think feelings are the same way. You've got to let them out when you're having them or you're just going to explode later on."

New-age psychobabble or not, Sabrina liked what Mr. Sheepshank was saying. She'd hadn't had an adult actually listen to her so well in a long time. In fact, he seemed almost eager to hear her thoughts.

"I think we'll forget all about this," the counselor continued. "You've been sitting here for several hours and have had plenty of time to think about what happened."

Sabrina got up from her seat, then paused and asked, "Mr. Sheepshank, does it get any better?"

He laughed. "I wish I could say it does, but don't worry, someday this place will be nothing but an ancient memory."

Sabrina looked up at the clock. School had been over for five minutes. Daphne would be waiting.

"I have to go meet my sister."

"Of course," Mr. Sheepshank said. "But before you go, I just want to remind you that my door is always open. I'm a pretty good listener."

Sabrina nodded. "I'll see you tomorrow, then," she said.

"I'm on the edge of my seat," the guidance counselor replied.

The girl nodded and stepped into the hallway. Natalie, the bully, was waiting by some lockers. Her left eye had a black-and-purple bruise around it. When she spotted Sabrina, she turned and punched a locker door. The impact was so great it dented the door badly. Happy with her handiwork, the big goon smiled, pointed at Sabrina, and shuffled down the hallway.

Great, I've been here less than eight hours and I already have a mortal enemy, Sabrina thought. *I wonder what Tuesday will be like?*

"Don't worry, Sabrina. Tomorrow's a new day," a voice behind her said. Sabrina spun around and found the pretty blond girl from her homeroom and gym class.

"That's what I'm worried about."

The girl laughed. "I'm Bella," she said. "And don't worry, not everyone's like Natalie."

Just then, Daphne rushed down the hallway to meet them. She had her coat and mittens on, and a couple of books under her arm.

"I've had the greatest day of my entire life!" she screamed as she hugged Sabrina tightly. "We spent the first part of the morning making papier-mâché hats, and then when the hats were dry we put them on and learned about what kind of people might have worn them. I had George Washington's hat."

The little girl paused to catch her breath.

"Daphne, this is Bella," Sabrina said, introducing the two. "She's in my homeroom."

"You made a friend?" Daphne said, giving her sister another hug. "Oh, I'm so proud of you!"

"Cute kid," Bella said, giggling. "I gotta get going. See you tomorrow."

Sabrina nodded and watched the girl disappear down the hallway. Maybe there was a chance of having a normal friend, after all.

"Did you know that George Washington didn't really have wooden teeth? That's a myth. Ms. White said his teeth were made from ivory and bone, 'cause . . ." Daphne paused and looked around. Then she cupped her hand around her sister's ear and finished her sentence. ". . . she actually knew him. But she didn't tell the class that, she just told me."

Then Daphne pulled away and returned to her normal, excited tone. "Then we learned all about chimpanzees. Did you know that chimpanzees aren't actually monkeys? I didn't know that. Chimpanzees are so punk rock."

"Punk rock?"

"You know, cool."

"Where did you hear that?" Sabrina laughed.

"Julie Melphy. She's in my class. She's very punk rock," her sister replied.

"That's stupid."

"You're stupid," Daphne shot back. "And very un-punk rock! How was your day?"

"Horrible," Sabrina grumbled. "Come on, I have to go get my coat from my locker. It's upstairs."

The girls climbed the steps to the second floor just as Toby came running down them. He nearly knocked them over.

"Out of the way, lightning-bolt head," he shouted then laughed his annoying little laugh. He ran past and disappeared down the hall.

That kid is so un-punk rock, Sabrina thought.

The sisters reached Sabrina's locker and she went to work on the combination. If there had been anything good about the day it was that at least she had been assigned a locker near her homeroom. She wouldn't have to trudge through the halls in the morning with all her books.

"What kind of class are you in?" Daphne asked as she peered through the window into Grumpner's room.

"What are you talking about?" Sabrina said as she put on her coat and closed her locker.

"Look," her sister said, pointing into Sabrina's homeroom.

Sabrina gazed through the window. The room looked as if a tornado had gone through it. Desks and chairs had been tossed around and there was an odd, white substance covering everything. She opened the door and the girls stepped inside. The white substance hung from the ceiling in strands like silky ribbons. It fluttered in the icy wind that blew in from a broken window. In the center of the room, a large sack of the junk was suspended from the ceiling, slowly swaying in the breeze.

"Don't touch anything," Sabrina said, tugging at a strand that had attached itself to her coat.

"What's that thing hanging from the ceiling?" Daphne asked as her sister crossed the room to look. Sabrina grabbed a nearby chair, pulled it close to the sack, and climbed onto the seat.

"Something's inside it," she said as she yanked at the layers of sticky stuff that formed the sack. Soon, something began to reveal itself from deep inside—something with a face. "It's Mr. Grumpner," she whispered. The old man was as purple as an eggplant and his once puffy face was gaunt and drained. "He's dead."

"Awww, man! That's so gross!" Daphne cried unhappily.

"What could have done this?" Sabrina wondered.

"Probably whoever left that," the little girl said, pointing at the far end of the classroom.

Sabrina turned to see what her sister was referring to. On the chalkboard was another horrible but familiar sight. Someone had dipped his or her hand into a can of paint and pressed it on the wall. The handprint was bright red.

4

The school doors flew open and a dark-haired man in a purple suit strutted in with his head in the air. He swaggered down the shiny hallway with a dwarf and an obese police officer bringing up the rear. When Sabrina spotted the group, she groaned. Mayor Charming was not one of her favorite people.

To anyone else, Mayor Charming might have seemed like a run-of-the-mill politician, but Sabrina knew better. Mayor Charming was really Prince Charming, the dashing romantic hero of a dozen fairy tales. But, as Sabrina knew firsthand, *Charming* was only his name. The mayor could be an obnoxious, rude know-it-all, and he had a particular disdain for Sabrina's family. In a nutshell, he hated the Grimms.

Racing to keep up was Mr. Seven, the mayor's diminutive side-kick. Seven was actually one of the original seven dwarfs and acted as Charming's driver, assistant, and whipping boy. Behind him was Sheriff Hamstead, who did his best to keep up with the others while trying to hoist his pants up at the same time.

"So, let's go through this one more time," the mayor said to his followers with an air of condescension. "Who's doing all the talking?"

"You are," Hamstead and Mr. Seven said in unison.

"And why is that?"

"Because we are numbskulls."

"See how easy that was?"

"But what if I see something suspicious? I am the sheriff, after all," Hamstead argued.

Charming came to a halt and spun around on his heels. "Are you going to make me get out the idiot hat? 'Cause it sounds like someone wants to wear the idiot hat!"

"I don't," Mr. Seven said.

The sheriff frowned and shook his head.

"Good," Mayor Charming snapped. He took a deep breath and looked up to the ceiling as if someone were watching from above. "OK, let's relax. Let out all the anger and frustration. You are a great mayor. Smile."

Suddenly, a smile sprang to Charming's face and he started down the hallway again. The mayor was a master at the phony, toothy grin, but it slid off his face when he spotted Sabrina and Daphne.

"What are they doing here?" he moaned.

"They found the body," the sheriff explained.

"The sisters Grimm found the body and no one told me?" Charming said.

"You told us not to talk," Mr. Seven said defensively.

The mayor bit down on his lower lip and mumbled a variety of curse words Sabrina had never heard before. He reached into his pocket, took out a folded piece of paper, and handed it to Mr. Seven, who looked down at it and frowned. The dwarf unfolded it, revealing a pointy paper hat, and put it on his head. Someone had written IDIOT in big black letters on the front of it. Mr. Seven lowered his eyes in humiliation.

"Howdy, Mayor," Daphne said happily. Even though Charming considered the Grimms his eternal enemies, Daphne had a soft spot for him. The mayor had helped the family stop Jack the Giant Killer, but most important, he had been kind to Elvis when the big dog was injured. Since then, the little girl had been convinced that deep down Mayor Charming was one of the good guys.

"Sheriff, let's make a new law. Children who cannot stay out of the way go to jail," he said through gritted teeth.

"You're so funny," Daphne said, smiling into the mayor's face. The little girl grabbed Charming's necktie, yanked him down to her level, and gave him a smooch on the nose. The anger melted from the man's face only to be replaced by confusion. He pulled away from the girl as if he had accidentally touched a hot stove.

Principal Hamelin rushed down the hall to join them. "Mayor Charming, Sheriff Hamstead, this is such a terrible tragedy. I just want you two to know that the faculty will cooperate in every way we can. I just feel horrible about this."

Charming smiled and shook the principal's hand, vigorously. "I appreciate that, Piper. We'll get to the bottom of this and be out of your hair as soon as possible," he said. "I assume you don't have any more of these running around the building?" He waved his hand at the girls as if he were trying to shoo away a couple of annoying houseflies.

"You mean children?" the principal said. "Oh, no. It happened at the end of the day and most of them were already on their way home."

"Sheriff, let's take a look," Charming said, gesturing to the door of Mr. Grumpner's classroom.

The two men tried to enter the room at the same time and

got jammed in the doorway together. They squirmed and shoved but were trapped until Mr. Seven came up from behind and pushed them into the room.

"I thought we weren't going to do that anymore," Mr. Charming said, maintaining his phony smile in front of everyone. Hamstead muttered an apology and immediately took a camera from his pocket. He snapped pictures of the unusual crime scene and Mr. Grumpner's disturbing corpse.

"He was found about ten minutes after the last bell," Principal Hamelin offered.

"I see," said Charming as he yanked some of the sticky stuff off a desk.

Sheriff Hamstead stepped close to the body to take more photos. He pulled aside a strand of the sticky substance to get a better look at Mr. Grumpner's face. "Looks like the blood has been drained right out of him."

"Maybe it was a vampire!" Daphne cried.

"There's no such thing as vampires," Charming muttered.

I used to think there was no such thing as you, Sabrina thought.

"Sheriff, do you have any idea what happened to him?" the principal asked.

"Well," Hamstead said as he put his camera away, "if I had to hazard a guess I'd say . . ."

"Spiders," Charming interrupted. "A whole bunch of spiders murdered him. There are so many cobwebs here I'd say it took hundreds of spiders to make them. Looks like they came in through the window."

"It's too cold for spiders," the sheriff argued, but when the mayor flashed him an angry look, the portly policeman zipped his lips.

"And what would the spiders' motivation be?" Sabrina asked.

"How should I know?" Charming said. "Maybe Mr. Grumpner stepped on one and its family wanted revenge."

"Spider revenge?" Sabrina asked.

"I don't hear anyone else with a better theory," Charming snapped.

Suddenly the door opened and Granny Relda and Mr. Canis entered the room.

"Oh, I have a theory," Granny Relda said, scanning the room. "It was a monster."

Daphne ran to the old woman and wrapped her arms around her.

"We found something gross," the little girl cried, burying her face into the old woman's bright green dress. Granny bent down and kissed her on the forehead.

"A monster!" Charming growled. "You've had some insane theories in the past, Relda, but monsters?"

"You're right, Mayor," the old woman said sarcastically. "Ferryport Landing has fairies, witches, robots, and men made out of straw, but monsters? Now I've really lost my marbles!"

Charming scowled. "Well, have your look around. I know I can't stop you."

"Thank you, Mayor," Granny Relda said. She crossed the room to Sabrina and took her by the hand. "Are you OK, *liebling*?"

Sabrina nodded.

Granny patted her on the head and walked over to the broken window. Among the glass was something long and black. The old woman gingerly moved the glass aside with her fingers and plucked the object off the ground. It was a feather.

"Gentlemen, I believe I have found a clue," she said.

Sheriff Hamstead took the feather and eyed it closely. "Looks like crow to me," he said. "There's a couple more there under the windowsill."

Mr. Canis took a deep sniff of the air. "It is crow."

"They probably blew in with the wind," Charming said, snatching the feather from the sheriff's pudgy hands. He tossed it to the floor as if it were meaningless.

"We found a clue, too!" Daphne said proudly. She pointed at the red hand painted on the chalkboard.

Hamstead, Charming, Mr. Seven, and Principal Hamelin peered at the red hand closely. Each of them had a worried look on his face.

"It's just like the one the police found in my parents' abandoned car," Sabrina said. "Or maybe that blew in with the wind, too."

Charming scowled and rolled his eyes at her. "Probably just a prank."

"A prank?" Sabrina and Daphne cried.

"Mayor Charming, that's the sign of the Scarlet Hand," said Granny Relda.

"There's no such thing as the Scarlet Hand," he said. "Hamstead has done a thorough investigation and we've concluded that Jack invented the whole thing."

Sabrina couldn't believe her ears. Charming knew the Scarlet Hand was real. He had admitted to the girls that the shadowy criminal group of Everafters had approached him. And this was before they'd heard Jack brag about being a member. Why was he now lying about its existence?

Before Sabrina could confront him, the door opened and Snow White entered. It didn't seem possible, but Ms. White was even more beautiful up close.

Mayor Charming rushed to block her view of Mr. Grumpner's corpse, but the teacher had already spotted it.

"So, it's true," she gasped.

"Snow, you shouldn't see this," Charming said softly.

"I'm fine," Snow White said, but the mayor ignored her. He took her by the hand and led her into the hallway. Sabrina and Daphne shared a glance and pushed through the crowd, eager not to miss a second of this royal soap opera.

The mayor pulled the teacher into his arms as if she needed comfort, and for a brief moment she seemed to enjoy it, but then she pulled away.

"Billy," Ms. White said, "what did that to him?"

"Try to put it out of your head, Snow," Charming said. He put his hand on her shoulder and looked deep into her eyes. It was hard to believe that the usually obnoxious mayor could be so tender. "I've got my best men on it."

The others filed out of Grumpner's classroom and Sheriff Hamstead took a roll of yellow police tape from his jacket. He draped an X over the door to keep anyone else from entering.

"Snow, I don't want you to get involved in this," the mayor said. The teacher flashed him an irritated look, but then nodded. She turned and bent down so that she was at eye level with Daphne.

"Are you OK?" she asked.

"Don't worry about me," the little girl answered. "We see this kind of thing all the time."

Mayor Charming turned to the sheriff. "Mr. Hamstead, could you make sure my fiancée . . . I mean Ms. White, gets home safely," he said, blushing over his mistake. As Snow White stood up she smiled softly, but the bright red blush on her cheeks flashed like a police siren on her pale skin.

"I'd be happy to," Sheriff Hamstead said, extending his arm to the beautiful woman. He escorted her down the hall and she stopped to gaze back at Charming before they left.

"So, what's next, *Billy?*" Sabrina said, before she burst into giggles. Daphne and Granny Relda joined her. Even Mr. Canis cracked a smile. Suddenly, a loud, goofy laugh was heard behind them. When they turned they found Mr. Seven nearly falling over with laughter.

"*Billy*," Sabrina continued. "That's just precious. It's so sweet I'm going to get a cavity."

"I think it's romantic," Daphne said, doing her best to stop laughing.

"Enough!" Charming shouted, silencing everyone's giggles. "This is a crime scene. Relda, take your rug rats and your mangy mongrel with you or I'll have you arrested."

"Watch your words, Prince," Canis growled as his eyes turned icy blue, showing everyone that the Wolf was just below the surface. "Someday you're going to wake up and find someone has taken a bite out of you."

"Relda, I believe there's a law in this town about keeping animals on a leash," Charming said.

The men stared at each other for a long moment and then, suddenly, Canis's eyes changed back to watery gray. The old man looked exhausted and his face grew pale.

"That's quite enough of this nonsense," Granny said, stepping in between the two men. Every time Charming and Canis were in a room together they were at each other's throats, but the old woman had a way of making them feel foolish. They stepped back and lowered their eyes like two squabbling schoolboys who had just been disciplined. "It's time to go."

The family exited the school and found their ancient black jalopy in the parking lot. The beat-up monstrosity was in desperate need of a tune-up and its long-neglected shocks groaned and complained as each person climbed inside. Elvis was in the back, snuggling under a huge blanket, and didn't even bother to lift his head when the girls got in. Daphne wrapped her arms around the dog's neck and gave him a big wet smooch on the forehead.

"I missed you today," she announced.

Elvis tucked his head under his blanket and hid.

"What's the matter with him?" the little girl asked.

"He's pouting. He doesn't like to be left in the car," Granny Relda said as she jotted something into her notebook.

"Awww, my little baby," Daphne said, trying to pull the two-hundred-pound dog onto her lap like an infant. She showered the Great Dane in kisses. "Is somebody sad? Did somebody get left in the car? I won't ever leave you in the car."

Elvis gave her a lick on the cheek and the girl giggled.

Granny spun around in her seat with a delighted look on her face. "*Lieblings*, you know what all this means?"

Sabrina groaned. "We're in the middle of a mystery?"

"Isn't it exciting?" the old woman cried.

"Yes, and pointless," the girl argued. "You heard Charming and his ridiculous spider theory. He knows the Scarlet Hand killed Mr. Grumpner, but instead he lies about it. Grumpner was a human, so Charming couldn't care less. Why should the Everafter mayor and the Everafter police department do anything at all? No, they'll just cover up his death, and we'll run into one dead end after another."

"We are Grimms and this is what we do," Daphne said.

"Exactly right, little one. We are Grimms and part of what we do is make sure that this kind of thing doesn't go unpunished. We'll just sit here until everyone is gone and then we'll go back inside and have a look ourselves," the old woman said. "I have a feeling there are a lot more clues in that room."

Suddenly, Mr. Seven was tapping on the car window. He motioned for Granny Relda to roll it down and looked around nervously.

"Good evening, Mr. Seven."

"Mayor Charming has requested your presence at the mansion."

"You mean *Billy*?" Granny said, turning in her seat to wink at the girls.

The dwarf chuckled. "He has something he wishes to discuss in private."

Granny Relda and Mr. Canis shared a suspicious glance. After a moment, Mr. Canis nodded his approval.

"Tell Mr. Charming we'll be there," the old woman said.

The dwarf nodded and walked over to the mayor's long white limousine. He buffed the silver stallion on the hood with his shirtsleeve then climbed onto the stack of phone books on the driver's seat, and soon the limo was pulling away.

"Are you sure you're feeling up to this?" Granny said, putting her hand on the old man's shoulder. Mr. Canis nodded. He started the car and it sputtered to life with a series of backfires that Sabrina was sure could be heard in the next town.

They followed Charming's limo through the quiet country roads of Ferryport Landing. Sabrina gazed out at the sleepy little river town that her great-great-great-great grandfather Wilhelm Grimm had founded. Anyone driving through it would think it was just another boring little town. They would never know that many of the residents were princes, pigs, witches, and fairies, all in disguise. And on the rare occasions when one of the really big Everafters caused trouble, such as one of the giants or dragons, the endless acres of firs, Chinese maples, and oak trees that surrounded the town acted as an excellent cover from prying eyes. In addition, the invisible magical barrier that Wilhelm and the witch Baba Yaga had constructed around Ferryport Landing meant no Everafter, no matter how big, could leave the area. As for the humans who lived in town, they were none the wiser. The Everafters were too good at covering up their magic and mischief. Sabrina often wished she were oblivious, too. Ferryport Landing was a perfect place to live, unless you knew that it was all a lie, and the lie kept Sabrina from getting comfortable in her new life.

As they pulled into Charming's sprawling estate, Sabrina realized the mayor was the only person in town she could trust. He was corrupt, but at least he was upfront about it. He planned to buy the town piece by piece and recreate the kingdom he had given up when the Everafters came to America. He didn't care if you liked it or not and he didn't care if you thought it was wrong. Charming could always be counted on to do what was right for himself. He might not have any morals, but at least he was consistent.

Mr. Canis parked the car and turned off the engine. The last time Sabrina had been at the mansion it had been lit up like a Christmas tree for the Ferryport Landing Ball, an annual event for which the Everafter community came together to be themselves and to celebrate. Without all the glitz and glamour, Charming's mansion looked vacant. The lights were off and the fountain, which featured a lifelike sculpture of Charming, was drained and full of dead leaves.

"Mrs. Grimm, if it's OK with you I believe I will stay here," Mr. Canis said as he opened the car door for Granny Relda. "I'm feeling a bit tired and I suspect Charming will only make it worse."

"Of course, Mr. Canis," Granny Relda said. "I don't believe Mayor Charming poses any threat to us."

Elvis whined when he saw that the family was leaving him in the car.

"Elvis, we're not leaving you in the car. We're putting you in charge of it," Daphne said. The dog lifted his huge ears as if he was listening very carefully. "It's a really important job. You have to stay and guard Mr. Canis. Don't let anything bad happen to him."

Elvis barked, confirming his orders. He sat up in the backseat and watched out the windows for any would-be attackers. As the Grimms approached the mansion, Sabrina looked back and noticed Canis doing something very odd. The stick-thin man climbed on top of the car and sat Indian-style on the roof. He closed his eyes and rested his hands on his knees.

"What's he doing?" Sabrina asked.

"Meditative yoga," Granny replied, as if this were the natural response. "It's helping him remain centered and calm. Keeps the dark stuff at bay."

Of course, the Big Bad Wolf does yoga, Sabrina thought. *Why did I even bother to ask?*

The trio stood on the front steps of the mansion, but before Granny could ring the bell, Mr. Seven opened the door and ushered the family inside.

"Good evening," he said and, without offering to take their coats, he turned and raced up the staircase. "I'll get the mayor."

"What do you think he wants?" Daphne wondered.

"Hard to say," Granny Relda said. "The mayor is full of surprises."

"Maybe he felt like he didn't get to insult us enough at the school," Sabrina muttered just as Charming appeared at the top of the steps. Sabrina watched him grimace, then take a deep breath as he came down to join them.

"This conversation must be an absolute secret," he said as he stood before them. He leaned down and pinned a shiny tin star on Sabrina's coat. It looked like the kind sheriffs wore in old black-and-white western movies. She peered down at it and read the words FERRYPORT LANDING SPECIAL FORCES DEPUTY OFFICER.

"What's this?" she asked as Charming pinned a similar star onto Daphne's coat. The little girl looked at it and smiled. "Look at me! I'm a cowboy!"

"May I?" Charming said to Granny Relda. The old woman hesitated but finally agreed and he pinned the star on her dress, too.

"I don't think I understand what is taking place, Mayor Charming," Granny Relda said.

"I'm deputizing you," he said uncomfortably. "Raise your right hand and repeat after me."

Charming raised his right hand and waited for the Grimms to do the same. Sabrina stared blankly at the man, wondering if maybe he was pulling some kind of prank on them.

"Don't make this harder on me than it has to be," he begged.

"The town needs your help. You know it and I know it. Can't that be enough?"

"You want our help?" Sabrina said.

"I know you've been helping Hamstead," the mayor said. "For some reason the sheriff thinks you will be able to help with this case."

"Mayor Charming!" Granny Relda exclaimed. "I never thought I'd see the day when you would come to this family for anything."

The man lowered his right hand and groaned. "Do you think I would ask you if it wasn't absolutely necessary? I swore I'd see your family rot before I asked for your help, but drastic times call for drastic measures."

"What are you talking about?" Sabrina demanded impatiently, but as she waited for the mayor to answer, she noticed something odd about the mansion. It was filthy. Several curtains in the ballroom had fallen and lay in heaps on the floor. A giant red stain had ruined a polar bear rug lying near the fireplace. The carpet on the stairs needed a good vacuuming and a bucket sat on the floor collecting rain from a giant patched-up hole in the ceiling. Half a dozen overflowing bags of garbage sat by the door waiting to be taken out and a thick layer of dust covered everything, including a full suit of armor that leaned precariously against a wall.

"What happened here?" she asked.

"You happened here!" Charming snapped. "You and your smelly sister ruined the only fund-raising event this town has each year."

Daphne raised an arm to smell her armpit. She crinkled her nose and lowered her arm quickly. "I'm not that bad," she said.

"You crashed an invitation-only party, brought a giant here, which nearly destroyed the mansion and several cars in the parking lot, and worst of all, you made me look like a fool in front of the town's biggest donors," the mayor said. "We didn't raise a penny. The town is broke."

"We know what the fund-raiser is *really* for," Sabrina replied. "You want to use the money to buy the whole town. Why don't you just dip into the money you've conned out of everyone for the last two hundred years?"

"You dare question my honor?" Charming growled. "I haven't taken a penny out of this town. The rumors about my finances are greatly exaggerated. Relda, do you believe I would live like this if I didn't have to?"

Granny Relda gazed around the room. "No, I don't," she answered.

"Services had to be cut drastically. Transportation, education. I've even had to fire the crew of workers who polish statues of me in the park. Mr. Seven has agreed to a substantial cut in pay and I haven't taken a salary in weeks. I had to lay off three-fourths of the town's police force, which, since there were only four police officers to begin with, leaves me with Hamstead. The sheriff works hard and he's smart as a whip, but he's only one pig. We're stretched too thin, and we just don't have the resources to investigate a crime, let alone a murder committed by the Scarlet Hand. I need your help, and since most of this is your family's fault, I think it's your responsibility."

"So now the Scarlet Hand exists, huh? Why did you lie about it back at the school?" Sabrina asked.

"Because I don't need the citizens of this town to panic. If word got out that there was a terrorist group killing people, there would be chaos in the streets. Hamstead can barely keep up now with speeding tickets and jaywalkers. Your family has proven to be good detectives: you're persistent and lucky and stubborn," Charming continued. "If *you* don't stop whatever did that to the teacher, then it won't get stopped."

"Why do you care what happens to a human teacher?" Sabrina said. "I thought you hated humans."

Charming said nothing.

"You don't want anything bad to happen to Ms. White," Daphne cried. "You are in love with her. You want to kiss and hug her!"

"Nonsense!" the mayor shouted. "I can't have terrorists running around the elementary school, even if I approve of who they're killing."

"You want to write her love notes," the little girl persisted. "You want to hold her hand in the park and look at puppies in the pet store."

"Is there an Off button for this one?" Charming asked Granny Relda.

The old woman grinned at the mayor. "You haven't answered the questions."

"All right!" Charming surrendered. "Snow has a knack for getting in trouble. I would sleep better at night knowing she is safe."

"Of course, we'll do what we can," Granny Relda assured him.

"What are you going to do for us?" Sabrina asked.

The old woman looked at the girl in horror. "*Liebling*, we would never take payment for helping folks."

"Granny, finding the killer is going to take a lot of time— time that we could use to find Mom and Dad," Sabrina argued.

"What can I do?" Charming said. "I can't exactly send Hamstead to search everyone's homes."

"No, but you have connections we don't," said Sabrina. "People *will* talk to you. *Maybe* there is something we could use, something magical lying around we don't know anything about. Use your imagination, *Billy*."

Charming thought for a moment. "You have my word."

He raised his right hand.

"It'll have to do," Sabrina said as she raised her hand as well. Granny Relda and Daphne did the same.

"I do solemnly swear to protect and serve the inhabitants of . . ."

"What does *inhabitants* mean?" Daphne interrupted.

"It means the people who live in a particular place," her sister answered, noting Charming's impatient face.

"Why didn't you just say *the people*, then?" the little girl asked.

"Let him finish, *lieblings*," Granny Relda said.

"I do solemnly swear," Charming started over, "to protect and serve *the people* of Ferryport Landing to the best of my ability. I vow to protect the peace, secure the safety, and uphold the rule of law."

The Grimms repeated what he said, word for word, and then lowered their hands.

"You are now officially deputized under the laws of Ferryport Landing," the mayor said, as he pulled out a set of keys and handed them to Granny Relda.

"What are these?" Granny said, looking down at the key ring.

"Keys to the school," Charming said. "You'll need them to get inside."

Granny smiled and handed the keys back to the mayor. "I've got my own set, thanks," she said. Charming scowled and shoved the keys back into his pocket.

"Well, I'd love to keep this happy event going all night, but as you know, I can't stand you people," he said, leading them to the door. As his hand clutched the knob, he turned and looked the girls in their eyes. "Snow is important to me. I would appreciate you keeping a close eye on her."

"No problem, *Billy*," Daphne replied, wrapping her arms around the mayor and hugging him tightly. "It's sooooo romantic!"

Charming sneered, opened the door, and forcefully shoved the family outside.

"You should really tell her that you love her," Daphne said, right before the mayor slammed the door in her face.

• • •

Sabrina had been to a lot of schools in the last year and a half, and they all had a few things in common. Every one of them had a couple of grouchy teachers, a bully, a bully's punching bag, a weird cafeteria lady, a bathroom that everyone was afraid to go into, and a librarian who worshiped something called the Dewey Decimal System. None of those schools, however, had a teacher-killing monster scurrying through its hallways. And they said New York City had everything.

Granny Relda was convinced that a monster—maybe working with the Scarlet Hand—had killed Mr. Grumpner. Not knowing exactly what the monster looked like or where it might be now was doing a number on Sabrina's nerves as her grandmother led the girls through the darkened hallways of the school. The long shadows cast by the setting sun looked like dinosaurs and invading aliens. Every little creak sounded like the tread of Bigfoot or a swamp monster. And worse, Grumpner's bloodless purple face appeared every time Sabrina closed her eyes. All she wanted to do was run back to the car and hide under Elvis's blanket, but Granny insisted they take another look at the crime scene. For once, the girl wished Mr. Canis was by their side, but the skinny old man had chosen to stay with the car and meditate in the freezing cold. Luckily, Granny had relented to Elvis's begging and the big dog now trotted down the hall beside them.

"Mr. Canis looks terrible, and for him, that's particularly bad," Sabrina said to the old woman as they crept along.

"In the past he has been able to tap into the Wolf's strengths without losing himself," her grandmother explained, "but this time he made a complete transformation and worse, he tasted human blood. It's been a very long time since that has happened and the Wolf is not going to be put away without a fight. Don't worry, children. Mr. Canis will win this battle."

"And if he doesn't?" Sabrina asked.

"He will. I'm sure he'll be happy that you are concerned for his well being."

I'm more concerned about waking up in his belly, Sabrina thought.

When they got to Sabrina's homeroom, the crime scene tape and Grumpner's body were already gone. The broken window had been replaced and all the cobwebs were cleared away. Even the blood-red hand painted on the chalkboard was gone. Other than some misplaced desks, there was no evidence of the gruesome scene they'd witnessed only hours before. Principal Hamelin had obviously cleaned the place up.

"Whatever it was didn't catch him by surprise," Granny Relda said, pushing a desk back into its row. "The way these desks are scattered it looks like Mr. Grumpner tried to fight back."

Sabrina shuddered as she imagined her teacher fighting off his attacker. Whether it was a giant spider or a thousand little ones, the fact was that the man's death had been a nightmare for him. Even a grouch like Grumpner didn't deserve to die so horribly.

"Why are we here now?" Daphne asked, as they walked into the classroom. "We'll never find anything in the dark."

"Some of the best clues are found in the dark," Granny said. She crossed the room and opened Grumpner's desk drawers. They were empty except for the bottom one. Inside was a picture of the teacher and a woman. They were on a pontoon boat enjoying an afternoon on the Hudson River. Grumpner and the woman each had a glass of champagne in their hands and were toasting each other.

"His wife?" Sabrina asked, as Granny showed her the picture. "I can't imagine that Mr. Cranky found anyone to marry him."

"He was probably a very different man at home," the old woman replied. "You told me once you thought your father was too careful, but the Henry Grimm I know threw caution to the wind. There are many sides to us all."

"His wife must be very sad." Daphne sighed.

Granny sighed, too. "I suppose she is."

"Well, we found a picture," Sabrina said, eyeing a shadow in the corner that looked like the boogie man. "Can we go now? This place is giving me the willies."

"Don't be scared," Daphne said. "I'm a police officer, ma'am. I'll protect you." She leaned down and struggled with her belt, then walked around the room mimicking Sheriff Hamstead's bowlegged gait.

Sabrina laughed so hard she snorted.

Granny reached into her handbag and pulled out a familiar pair of infrared goggles. "Don't worry, *lieblings*, I'm hurrying," she said as she put the goggles over her eyes and looked around the room, finally focusing on the floor. "Ah-ha! Children, come and take a look."

The girls hurried to their grandmother. Daphne took the goggles and looked down at the floor. "That is so punk rock!" she said.

Eager for a turn, Sabrina snatched the goggles away from her sister and peered through their special lenses. They revealed ghostly white footprints—the last traces of the late Mr. Grumpner.

Granny Relda reached down and ran her finger across the floor. When she lifted it, there was white powder on it. "The plot thickens," she said, holding her chalky finger up to Sabrina's eyes. "Mr. Grumpner's feet were covered in some kind of dust."

A bit of the dust floated up into Sabrina's nose and she sneezed violently.

"Gesundheit," Granny Relda said.

"They come from out in the hallway," Sabrina said, opening the door and following the glowing footprints.

"Notice anything about the steps?" her grandmother asked, following closely behind.

"They're very far apart," the girl said. "Three of my steps are equal to about one of his."

"That's because he was running," the old woman informed her. Sabrina was impressed. Granny Relda was a natural detective, and Sabrina wondered if she'd ever be as smart. The footprints came from the stairs to the first floor and the girl headed in that direction until suddenly the infrared goggles were snatched off her head.

"Hey!" she complained, as she turned on her little sister. "If you wanted to wear them, all you had to do was ask!"

Granny and Daphne said nothing. They were looking at the ceiling with odd expressions. Sabrina followed their gaze and what she saw sent a shock down to her toes. Hanging upside down above them was a fat, frog-faced creature. Its head and feet were amphibious, with slimy, bumpy skin and a puffed, bulbous pouch under its lower lip, but it had the arms, legs, and body of a human being. It was the creature's long sticky green tongue that had snatched the goggles off Sabrina's head, and now it dragged them in and out of its mouth as if it were wondering whether they might make a good snack. Eventually it spit them out at Sabrina's feet, spraying sticky saliva all over the girl's pants.

"Uh, no thanks. You can keep them," Sabrina said, wiping the goop off her jeans.

The frog monster let out an odd, feminine giggle, and puffed up its huge air sack. Sabrina had seen frogs do just the same thing on TV. It was something they did when they were preparing to eat and she suddenly had the feeling that she was on the menu.

"Run!" she cried.

The Grimms and Elvis spun around and ran back down the hallway, but the monster leaped off the ceiling and landed in front of them, blocking their path.

"I spy with my little eye," the frog-girl gurgled, "something dead."

5

Granny Relda swung her handbag at the frog-girl and cracked her on her forehead. The monster groaned and fell to the ground. Sabrina had seen what sort of stuff the old woman kept in her purse—everything from spy goggles to rolls of quarters—so she knew it packed quite a wallop. It would take the frog-girl a while to get up—if she got up at all.

Not wasting any time, the Grimm women spun in the opposite direction and raced down the stairs. Elvis followed close behind, clumsily navigating the steep steps and barking threateningly.

"If we're lucky," Granny Relda said through winded breaths, "that thing will be too afraid of Elvis to come after us."

"And if we aren't?" Sabrina asked as she helped her grandmother down the last of the steps. Unfortunately, the old woman didn't get a chance to respond. The frog-girl bounced down the steps and onto a nearby wall, sticking like a suction cup.

Elvis stood his ground, baring his teeth at the monster, daring her to come closer.

"Your puppy isn't very nice," the frog-girl croaked. "But he'll digest in my belly as quickly as the three of you."

Daphne stepped forward and flashed her shiny new deputy's badge. "You're under arrest for . . . for . . . being gross!" she stammered, but the frog-girl was not impressed. She lunged for the little girl.

Sabrina grabbed her sister's hand and dragged her down the hallway toward the exit. The monster followed by leaping back and forth from wall to wall, gaining ground with each jump. By the time the Grimms reached the exit, the frog-girl was right behind them. She shot her thick tongue out and wrapped it around Daphne's arm, dragging the little girl back into her clutches.

Elvis leaped viciously at the creature, but it jumped to the ceiling and hung upside down out of his reach.

"Let her go!" Sabrina shouted as she desperately reached for her sister. The frog-girl let out a sickening giggle and continued to dangle Daphne right above Sabrina's grasp. The little girl struggled and squirmed and finally reached into her beehive hairdo. She yanked a protractor from her sticky locks and stabbed the frog's tongue with it. The monster shrieked and Daphne fell, knocking Sabrina to the ground.

"And you didn't like my hairdo," Daphne said to her sister as she quickly helped her to her feet and the two ran to the exit doors with Granny Relda and Elvis close behind.

"Start the car!" Sabrina shouted as they sprinted across the school lawn. Mr. Canis opened his eyes and, without pausing, climbed off the roof of the car. Within seconds the old jalopy roared to life, grinding metal on metal and shaking violently. The junker's obnoxious concert had never sounded so good to Sabrina.

"What happened?" Mr. Canis asked as Elvis, Granny, and the girls clamored into the car, but no one got to answer. Something slammed onto the roof. It was so loud they all jumped, except Mr. Canis, whose only reaction was to look up and raise a questioning eyebrow.

Just then, a slimy green hand smacked the driver's side window. Sabrina and Daphne screamed. Granny Relda whooped in astonishment and Elvis growled and bared his teeth. But Mr. Canis just took a deep breath, put the car into drive, and floored the gas. The car's tires squealed and the jalopy rocketed into the street, skidding across the country road before some quick steering set it on the right course.

"Oh, I do wish I could drive." Granny Relda groaned. "I used to love situations like this."

"You know very well the police took your license away," Mr. Canis said, steering from one side of the road to the other in hopes of dislodging their stowaway. Unfortunately, nothing the old man did had any effect on the monster and it continued to beat violently on the roof.

"I got a couple of speeding tickets." Granny shrugged.

"You were arrested fourteen times for reckless endangerment. Several neighborhood groups banned you from driving on their streets. The German government said that if they ever caught you in a car in Berlin again you would be hanged," the old man corrected.

"Oh, Mr. Canis," Granny begged. "No one has to know. Besides, this isn't getting us anywhere."

He shook his head.

"Please!" she pleaded.

Mr. Canis slammed his foot on the brake and the car screeched to a halt. The frog-girl tumbled down the hood and bounced along the road for several yards until she stopped. She let out a terrible moan and then lay still.

"Let's stay off the major roads," the old man said, opening his door and getting out.

Granny squealed with delight and scooted over to the driver's seat. As they switched places, Sabrina watched the grotesque frog-girl stir, slowly get to her feet, and stare at the car. Even with her bizarre, twisted face, the murderous rage in her eyes was clear.

"Children," Mr. Canis said as he turned to face the sisters. "Put on your seat belts."

The girls eyed each other nervously and hurried to strap themselves in. Unfortunately, the ancient seat belts that had been installed in the car were torn, so Mr. Canis had used ropes to improvise. Sabrina helped Daphne tie hers into a knot around her waist and then went to work on her own.

Just as their ropes were secure, the monster leaped into the air and came down violently on the car's front end. The impact was so great, the car's back end lifted a full six feet off the ground, then came down violently. The monster leaned forward to get a better look through the windshield and then licked her wide lips.

"Going somewhere?" She laughed.

Elvis whined and crawled under his blanket as Granny floored the accelerator and the car lunged forward. The monster tumbled over the hood, up the windshield, over the roof, onto the trunk, and fell off the back end of the car.

"She's gone!" Sabrina cried, just before the freak hopped back onto the trunk. It laughed at them through the rear window.

"She's back," Daphne cried, diving under the blanket with Elvis.

Granny made a sharp left onto an old dirt road and pressed hard on the gas pedal. The ancient car screamed in protest, but held up its end with a burst of speed so powerful Sabrina felt the g-force pushing her body into the seat springs. Despite the incredible speed, the frog-girl held on with little effort and pounded angrily on the rear window. The massive blows caused a thick crack in the glass.

"Turning right!" Granny shouted from the driver's seat, just before she made the turn. Elvis tumbled over the girls as the car banked to the right, but the maneuver didn't seem to shake the monster.

"Turning left!" Granny shouted and Elvis tumbled to the other side of the car, landing heavily on Sabrina's belly and knocking the wind out of her.

The frog-girl smacked the window again, and this time it exploded, sending chunks of glass into the backseat. Several large

portions of the window stayed attached, but the monster pulled them off effortlessly and tossed them into the road.

Sabrina pushed Elvis off of her and fought to fill her empty, burning lungs. As she struggled, the frog-girl reached into the backseat with her big sticky hands, unfastened Daphne's rope belt, and snatched the little girl right out of her seat. Still choking and gasping for air, Sabrina grabbed desperately at Daphne's ankle and tried to pull her back inside the car, but the frog-girl's grip was too strong.

"She's got Daphne," she gasped, but Mr. Canis had already sprung into action. He rolled down his window and pulled his upper body out of the car.

"There's no need to hurry, old man," the frog-girl screamed over the wind. "You'll die soon enough."

A ferocious roar echoed back at the monster and Sabrina could see her eyes grow wide with surprise.

"You're one of us?" the frog-girl cried. "And you fight for the life of a filthy Grimm! You're the traitor. I should have known you by your stink."

"Put the child back into the car," Sabrina heard Mr. Canis demand, even over the roaring engine.

"The traitor gets no favors!" The frog-girl laughed. She reached into the backseat with her free arm and grasped for

Sabrina. Sabrina squirmed and slapped at the disgusting hand, but it still managed to snatch her sweater and drag her out the window as well.

"I'm not going to tell you again, beast," Mr. Canis threatened.

"I've heard stories about you, traitor," the monster croaked. "The Big Bad Wolf—trying to make amends for all the bad things he has done. You'll fail, old-timer! Your heart isn't in it! But no matter, I'll give you the dignity of knowing you died trying!"

Mr. Canis was too far away to do anything. Sabrina knew if she and her sister were going to survive, they were going to have to save themselves.

"Daphne, do you remember Mr. Oberlin?" Sabrina shouted, hoping her sister had not forgotten this particular foster father.

"From the Bronx?" the little girl asked.

Sabrina nodded.

The disgusted look flashing across her sister's face told Sabrina that her plan wasn't the little girl's favorite. Regardless, Daphne nodded and together the sisters leaned down and bit the frog-girl hard.

The monster shrieked in agony and let go of Daphne. Sabrina grabbed her sister and together they scrambled back into the car. The frog-girl huddled on the trunk, clutching her wounds.

"What happened?" Granny Relda said, still pushing hard on the gas.

"It appears I am not the only one in our home with fangs," Mr. Canis said, climbing back into the car.

"You've got to get rid of this thing," Sabrina shouted as she wiped the horrible taste out of her mouth with her shirtsleeve. A bit of the goo was on her chin and her shirt stuck to it like it was a powerful glue. Daphne was also busy rubbing the monster's taste off her tongue onto her sleeve. Again, the frog-girl reached in through the window, but Elvis snapped at her hand and the monster pulled it back.

"Don't worry, *lieblings*," Granny said as she made a rough turn onto a gravel road. "I have a plan."

Sabrina looked through the windshield and saw a sign blocking the road ahead. It read DANGER! BRIDGE UNSAFE! GO NO FARTHER! Worse was what was beyond it. In the distance was an old, rundown country bridge covering a rocky stream. One look at it told Sabrina that a mouse wouldn't be able to cross the bridge safely, let alone Granny Relda's ancient two-ton monstrosity on wheels.

"What's Granny's plan?" Daphne said, smacking at the frog monster's hand as it snatched at her through the window.

"You don't want to know!" Sabrina replied.

The car crashed through the old wooden sign and it exploded around them. A giant chunk slid over the roof and by the sound of the pained groan, smacked the monster in her head. The collision was enough to knock the frog-girl off the car and she tumbled painfully to the ground.

Unfortunately, Granny didn't stop driving, and when the jalopy raced onto the beginning of the rickety bridge, Sabrina knew they were in trouble. Creaking beams and snapping wood drowned out the car's backfires and grinding gears. The old bridge tilted to the left just as the car reached the halfway point, and she saw a sight that nearly gave her a heart attack. The middle of the bridge had collapsed, leaving a giant hole no car could ever get across. And Granny wasn't slowing down.

"Granny, we're not going to make it!" Sabrina shouted, battling the roaring engine to be heard.

"I love pancakes, too," the old woman shouted back.

I hate this car, Sabrina thought to herself.

Granny Relda floored the accelerator, the engine screamed, a flame shot out of the car's muffler, and suddenly they were soaring over the gaping hole. They landed hard on the other side and raced onto the road just as the bridge buckled and collapsed into the rocky stream below.

After several yards, Granny brought the car to a stop. She shut off the engine.

"That took care of the ugly little beast." Granny laughed as she turned around to face the girls. "How exciting was that? Were you excited? I'm having the time of my life!"

Everyone remained speechless, except for Elvis, who whined softly. Granny Relda didn't notice; she continued to jabber on like a little kid who had had too much sugar before bedtime.

"Oh, boy, did Froggie get the surprise of her life," she continued, smacking the steering wheel proudly. "You put Relda Grimm behind the wheel and things get done."

The old woman turned back around and prepared to start the car again but everyone shouted *"No!"* in unison. Mr. Canis snatched the keys out of the ignition. Sabrina saw the disappointment in her grandmother's face. The old woman slowly got out of the car and Mr. Canis slid over into the driver's seat. As she got in on the passenger's side, Granny Relda crossed her arms and pouted. It reminded Sabrina of something Daphne would do.

"My driving isn't that bad, is it?" the old woman asked.

"Yes!" everyone shouted.

• • •

Once the house was unlocked, the family staggered inside, with Sabrina quietly cursing one of the worst days of her life.

Puck was sprawled across the couch. He had moved the books away from the television and was watching it with the sound all the way up. The boy was surrounded by three delivery pizza boxes, empty bags of chips, a leaky carton of ice cream, and a two-liter bottle of soda from which he was currently drinking. On his belly was a can of spray cheese and when he saw the family limp into the house, he put down the soda and lifted the cheese can, spraying an enormous portion into his mouth. Then he gargled with it. Once he had swallowed the greasy orange junk food, he let out an enormous belch that actually rattled the windows.

"Old lady!" he crowed. "You've been hiding this magic box from me! You can see other worlds on it. I just watched a man and his talking sports car jump across a river!"

Sabrina felt her exhaustion turn instantly to anger. From their expressions, she could see the rest of the family felt the same way. While they had been hunted by a frog monster, Puck had had the best day of his life. Fate was cruel.

"What?" he said defensively, noticing their glares.

Granny started dinner and patiently explained to Puck what had happened to them. The boy seemed to think Mr. Grumpner's murder was fascinating and was terribly depressed that he hadn't seen the frog-girl.

"Was she ugly?" he asked. "Why is it that I miss all the fun?"

"I guess you just don't have our luck," Sabrina grumbled.

"I hope the two of you washed," he said to the girls. "Frogs give you warts and it sounds like the one you fought off was mighty big. I wouldn't be surprised if you wake up in the morning and find you are one giant brown wart."

Daphne's eyes grew as big as saucers. "Nuh-uh," she said.

"Sorry, kiddo, but if you hurry and take a bath it might not be too late!" Puck advised.

The little girl rushed out of the kitchen and could be heard running through the house and up to the bathroom.

"You shouldn't tease her like that," Sabrina said, vigorously washing her hands at the kitchen sink.

"Puck, do you know the Widow?" Granny Relda asked as she got up to stir a pot of soup on the stove.

"Of course," Puck replied. "Queen of the crows."

"Go get her," Granny Relda said.

"Why?" he asked. "Are we going to cook her?"

"Of course not," Granny said, horrified. "I have some questions for her."

"Since when does the Trickster King act as your messenger, old lady?" the boy asked.

"Since he started living under her roof," Mr. Canis growled.

He slammed his fist down hard on the kitchen counter, causing the sugar bowl to lose its lid. "This is serious business, boy. Now go!"

Puck eyed Canis stubbornly. "Villains do not run errands!"

The old man's eyes turned ice blue and a bit of his Wolf voice came out. "I'll show you a villain, Trickster."

Glistening wings sprang from Puck's back and flapped loudly. He flew quickly through the house and slammed the front door as he left.

Mr. Canis leaned against the kitchen doorway and tried to catch his breath. This was the first day he had been out of his room in three weeks and it hadn't been an easy one. If the old man was struggling with keeping his emotions in check, the last four hours had been an incredible test.

"Mr. Canis," Granny said, rubbing the old man's back with her palm. "Go and rest."

"There may be more danger," Canis insisted.

"Old friend, I already have three children arguing all the time," Granny Relda scolded, "I do not need another."

The old man nodded and shuffled out of the kitchen.

"Who's the Widow?" Sabrina asked.

"Hans Christian Andersen wrote about her in 'The Snow Queen.' She's an old friend," Granny said. "She might be able to shed some light on the crow feathers we found. She's sort of an expert on birds."

"So you don't think the frog-girl killed Mr. Grumpner?" Sabrina said.

"No, *liebling*, frogs don't make webs," the old woman said.

"Neither do birds."

"True. But the birds may have seen something."

• • •

When dinner was ready, Granny and the girls met in the dining room. Daphne's skin was red from scrubbing and her hair was wrapped up in a big white towel. The family took their seats and Granny served herself and the girls some hot soup and buttered rolls. The soup tasted like warm butterscotch pudding but Sabrina was so hungry she didn't have the strength to make her usual complaint about her grandmother's weird food.

Between slurps of soup, the old woman jotted some notes in her notebook.

"Well, then, it looks like we've got two monsters on our hands, now," Granny Relda said. "One frog-girl . . ."

"An a ian ida," Daphne mumbled between bites of bread.

"What?'

Daphne swallowed. "And a giant spider," she repeated and then immediately stuffed another oversized bite into her mouth.

"I agree," Granny Relda said. "Charming was way off on his 'army of spiders' theory. I think it was one big one."

"Don't forget the broken window," Sabrina said. "That's how it got inside."

"Maybe," Granny replied.

"You don't think so?" the girl asked.

"The glass was all over the floor, so something came through that window, and by how spread out the shards of glass were, I'd say it came in fast."

"Urds," Daphne mumbled, with a mouthful of soup.

"Right, the birds," Sabrina said. "The black feathers were underneath the window. But that's where I get confused. Why would birds have come into the room?"

"Birds eat spiders," Granny Relda explained as she stood up and crossed the room to a pile of books stacked next to the radiator. She tugged at a couple in the middle of the stack and sent the rest tumbling to the ground. She left the fallen pile where it was and returned to the table. Granny wasn't much of a housekeeper.

"This book is just about everything ever written on giant monster spiders," Granny Relda said, setting it in front of the girls. "It's a bit dry, and the author has an unhealthy fear of certain animals, but it might be helpful."

Sabrina eyed the book, entitled *Magical Mutations of Insects,*

Reptiles, and Kitties. She opened the cover and saw a crude drawing of a giant kitten chewing on several screaming farmers. She flipped to another page and a thin pamphlet fell out. She picked it up and examined it. The cover read *Rumpelstiltskin's Secret Nature.*

"What's this?" she said, leafing through it. The pages were filled with tiny, neat writing.

"I've been looking for that for ages," Granny said. "That's a book your great aunt Matilda Grimm wrote."

Daphne took the pamphlet. "Rumpel . . . rumpel . . . what's this say?"

"It's called *Rumpelstiltskin's Secret Nature,*" her grandmother said, taking the booklet from the little girl. "Matilda wrote a lot about Rumpelstiltskin. You could say she was one of the few fairy-tale specialists in this family. She had dozens of theories on why Rumpelstiltskin kept trying to trick people out of their first-born children. You should read it when you get a chance."

"I'll check this out later," Sabrina said, setting the mutations book aside.

"Anyone for more camel hump soup?" Granny Relda asked as she got up from the table.

"This is made from a camel's hump?" Sabrina cried, dropping her spoon as images of a sweaty, flea-covered camel danced around in her mind. She'd seen one at the Bronx Zoo with her father and could still smell its rank breath years later. She felt sick.

"Actually, it's two-hump camel soup but I only use the second hump," Granny Relda explained. "The first hump is a little tough, and besides, it's the second hump that has all the flavor."

The girls stared at the old woman as if she were playing an elaborate joke on them, but Sabrina could see from her expression that she was serious. Of course, Daphne clapped her hands happily, and cried, "I'll have more! And this time make sure there's some extra hump in there!"

Sabrina slowly pushed her nearly empty bowl away just as there was a knock on the front door. Granny, who was on her way to the kitchen, stopped and rushed to answer it, with the girls following right on her heels. There on the porch stood a humongous black crow. Its eyes and beak bobbed nervously, and its squawk was ear-shattering. On one of its legs was a black ribbon, and when it saw the family it dipped its head in what Sabrina guessed was a bow of respect.

"Good afternoon, Widow," Granny Relda said to the bird.

"Good afternoon to you, Relda Grimm," the crow croaked in a scratchy yet feminine voice. Daphne squealed in glee, but Sabrina's stomach did a flip-flop.

More talking animals, ugh.

"Do you know that little brat you sent plucked a feather out of my behind and laughed?" the crow continued.

"I am very sorry," Granny Relda apologized. "I haven't seen you as a crow in some time."

"Well, the boy said it was important, so I did the bird thing. Normally, I'd take the seven down to the forty and get off at Miller Road, but you know that disaster with all the orange cones, and right now the eighteen is backed up for miles. At this time of night flying is really the quickest way," the bird croaked.

"Your English is coming along very well," Granny Relda commented.

"Thank you," the crow cawed. "Some of the others refuse to speak anything but Crow-ish, but I say you have to adapt. It's good to learn new things. I've even been surfing the Web."

"What fun," Granny said with a smile. "I was wondering if you had heard about the human that was killed today at the elementary school?"

"Yes, I have," the Widow replied. "Want to know how I know?" Granny nodded.

"A little bird told me," the crow said. For a moment, there was silence. "Get it? *A little bird told me?*"

"That's very funny," the old woman said, as a pained smile

crossed her face. Sabrina rolled her eyes, but Daphne laughed so hard she snorted.

"Oh, I like the little one." The crow chuckled. "You gotta have a good sense of humor to live in this town."

"The death was very suspicious," Granny Relda said, trying to steer the conversation back to the murder. She took one of the black feathers they had found in the classroom out of her handbag and held it out to the bird. "This was at the crime scene."

"I've heard rumblings in the flock," the Widow said, eyeing the feather.

"Rumblings?" Granny Relda asked.

The bird hesitated and looked around as if someone might be listening.

"Some of the crows claim they blacked out. They say they can't account for about fifteen minutes of the day," the crow whispered. "The ones I talked to said they heard music and suddenly they were all standing around the school yard, unsure of how they got there. Sounds like the piper is back to his old games."

"That would be unfortunate," Granny said.

"But I don't think it's your biggest problem," the crow continued. "Someone's sent you a message and I'm warning you, Relda, you don't want to mess with the Scarlet Hand."

"I don't know what you're talking about," said the old woman. "What message?"

"It's all over your house, Relda. Whatever you've gotten involved in this time has attracted the attention of some very bad people."

Sabrina and Daphne ran down the porch steps and looked up at the house. On the windows, roof, and even on the chimney were red-paint hands, just like the one they had found on the chalkboard in Mr. Grumpner's room.

"Who did this?" Sabrina asked.

"We've only been home for an hour," Daphne added.

The Widow hopped down the steps and flew up into the air. "Keep your nestlings close," the crow squawked as it disappeared over the tree line.

"Girls, get back into the house," Granny Relda said sternly.

6

t was obvious to Sabrina that the Scarlet Hand had spooked Granny Relda. The old woman spent the rest of the night silently digging through her old books and taking notes. When the girls announced they were going to bed, she mumbled what sounded like *good night*, but kept researching.

While Daphne brushed her teeth, Sabrina ran her head under the bathtub faucet and washed her hair for the fourth time that day. She wrapped it up in a towel, and the girls headed for their bedroom. Daphne put on her favorite pair of footie pajamas and pinned her deputy's badge to them. After buffing it into a shine, she went to their father's desk, which the little girl was slowly converting into a beauty parlor, and took a hairbrush from one of its drawers.

"Can I?" she asked. Sabrina nodded and her little sister climbed up on the bed, took the towel off of the older girl's head, and ran the brush over her long blond hair. For some reason, brushing Sabrina's hair helped calm Daphne down so that she could go to sleep. After finding a dead body, being attacked by a frog-girl, nearly dying with Granny behind the wheel of the car, and having the house vandalized right under their noses, Daphne would be brushing for a long time, Sabrina suspected.

"You OK?" she asked.

"I can't get Mr. Grumpner's face out of my head," Daphne replied.

"Try not to think about it."

"But we have to think about it. Now that we're police officers, it's up to us to find his killer."

"I think we should let the sheriff handle this one," Sabrina said.

"We can't. We made a vow. Besides, the town needs us to solve the mystery. We are Grimms and this is what we . . ."

"What we need to *do* is find Mom and Dad," Sabrina interrupted.

"We'll find them," her sister said.

"I don't know how. We've been here for three weeks and have

spent all our time catching Lilliputians and killing giants. Isn't it time to start putting Mom and Dad first?"

"The mayor needs our help."

"And while we're busy doing the mayor's job, Mom and Dad are still missing," Sabrina snapped. "How do we know that Charming isn't responsible?"

"He wouldn't do that."

"He's an Everafter, Daphne! Everafters can't be . . ."

"What?" Daphne said. "Everafters can't be what?"

"Trusted!" Sabrina exploded.

Her sister looked at Sabrina as if she didn't recognize her. It was an expression more hurtful than any word the little girl could have said.

"It's obvious an Everafter kidnapped our parents and it's also obvious that an Everafter is behind Grumpner's murder," Sabrina tried to explain.

"Sabrina, they aren't all bad."

"All the ones I've met," the older girl insisted.

Daphne set the hairbrush on the nightstand, crawled under the covers, and turned her back on her sister.

"I don't like you very much, right now," she whispered.

"You'll see I'm right soon enough," Sabrina said.

She stared up at the ceiling, waiting for Daphne to respond, but the little girl remained quiet. Sabrina told herself she didn't care. Daphne wasn't going to make her feel guilty. She'd worry about being tolerant and accepting when their mother and father came home.

"Good night," she whispered, but her sister said nothing. Sabrina snatched a copy of *The Blue Fairy Book* off the night-stand and opened it to page one. Maybe there was something in the book, some kind of magic she could use to find their parents.

• • •

Once the house was quiet, Sabrina grabbed her set of keys up from under the bed, snatched a book off her nightstand, and headed to Mirror's room. When she walked through the portal, she found him with a reflective silver card under his chin and a tanning lamp shining in his face. On a nearby table he had a pitcher of margaritas and a bottle of suntan lotion. When he saw Sabrina, he smiled and flicked off the lamp.

"Just in time, kiddo," the little man said. "I'm roasting over here. How was your first day of school?"

"Oh, the usual. The kids made fun of me, I punched a bully, and a teacher was murdered by a monster," Sabrina replied.

"Sixth grade isn't how I remember it," Mirror said, reaching over to a table and pouring himself a fresh drink. "Sorry, I'd offer you one but you're a bit young. How about a Shirley Temple?"

"No thanks," Sabrina said.

"I remember my school days. It wasn't easy for a shy talking mirror, but I managed. Trust me, starfish, it gets better the day after."

"The day after what?"

"The day after you graduate," Mirror said. "Are you feeling OK? You look flushed."

"I think I'm getting sick," the girl said, holding her hand to her forehead to check for a fever. "I've been getting headaches all day and I've been a cranky jerk to almost everybody."

"Sounds like puberty to me. If you think school is tough now, wait until you start getting zits."

"So, you're sure I'm not sick?"

"Completely, kiddo. I remember when your dad went through it. He was in a fistfight every day for two weeks. I remember one time he got your grandfather so angry the old man chased him up a tree." Mirror laughed.

"So, this is normal," Sabrina said. "I thought I was going crazy."

"I didn't say you weren't going crazy," the little man responded.

"I just said you were growing up. The two are not mutually exclusive. So, did you just come to chat or are we going on a magic hunt again tonight?"

Sabrina sheepishly held out a book about King Arthur's powerful wizard, Merlin.

"Come on, kiddo," Mirror said, sounding resigned, and Sabrina followed him down the hall.

• • •

Early the next morning, Sabrina awoke to a thundering racket, followed by a series of thuds and crashes that knocked a picture off her bedroom wall. Something was going on at the end of the hallway that sounded like a fistfight and Sabrina knew there could be only one source of the chaos—Puck. She eyed the clock and saw that it was only five a.m. and her blood began to boil. Five a.m. was too early for his nonsense.

Of course, Daphne slept through the noise, snoring away as if nothing was happening. The little girl could sleep through World War Three. The only thing she wouldn't sleep through was breakfast.

Sabrina leaped out of bed and marched down the hallway. The day before had taught her not to just barge into his room, so she banged on the door angrily instead. After several moments, she realized that the tremendous noise she heard wasn't coming from inside Puck's bedroom, but from the bath-room down the hall. Fearing her grandmother had fallen in the tub, Sabrina rushed to the bathroom door, grabbed the knob, and flung the door open just as a nearly naked eleven-year-old boy ran past her.

"Puck!" Granny Relda cried. "Come back here!"

Mr. Canis leaped to his feet and rushed past Sabrina, chasing the boy, who had fled downstairs.

"What's going on?" the girl asked, as she peered into the bath-room. It was a complete disaster. The bathtub was surrounded by a dozen empty bottles of shampoo and what looked like the wrappings of at least twenty bars of soap. The inside of the tub was filled with an oily black sludge that slowly spiraled down the drain. On the toilet basin was a plate where four fat worms, sev-eral dead beetles, a hand grenade, and thirty-six cents in change had been collected.

"Puck is having his bath . . . his eighth bath," Granny Relda said, partly exhausted and partly annoyed. "You've let him out and now he's probably in the woods rolling in who knows what . . . *again*!"

"He's taking a bath?" Sabrina said. Puck hadn't taken a bath since he'd moved into the house and his unbearable stink had ruined many a meal for the girl. One whiff of his nauseating aroma was all anyone needed to realize that the Trickster King and soap were bitter enemies.

"Not that I'm complaining, but why is he taking a bath?" she asked suspiciously.

"We felt it was necessary, under the circumstances," said Granny Relda. Sabrina noticed the old woman was wearing plastic gloves to protect her hands.

"Circumstances? What circumstances?"

But Granny's explanation was interrupted by Mr. Canis, who stomped back up the stairs with the boy in his arms. Puck squirmed and kicked the entire way.

"This is rubbish!" he shrieked as the old man dragged him back into the bathroom and wrapped him in a clean towel.

"The tub is clogged again," Granny Relda said. "I suppose we could try another round on the teeth while it drains."

Sabrina eyed the bathroom sink where four worn-down and abused toothbrushes had met their doom. Several tubes of toothpaste littered the floor. Each had been thoroughly emptied of all its cavity-fighting protection.

"Will someone please tell me what is going on in here?" Sabrina demanded.

Puck turned and smirked at the girl. A devilish gleam sparkled in his eyes and he temporarily ceased his indignant protests.

"Guess what, piggy! I'm going to school with you today!" he shouted as he kicked the door closed in her face. "I'm going to be your bodyguard!"

• • •

"Yes, you absolutely do need a bodyguard." Granny Relda argued with Sabrina as she tried to pat Daphne's hair down with her hand. The little girl had molded her still glue-soaked locks into a pointy Mohawk that stood about a foot and a half above her head. Finding little success, Granny gave up and turned her attention to serving each girl glow-in-the-dark waffles for breakfast. "We've got two monsters running around in the hallways."

"But why him?" Sabrina cried. Her own hair had become super curly after her multiple shampoos, producing an almost perfect globe shape, like a big yellow tennis ball. "Why don't *you* come?" she said to her grandmother. "You could use a fairy godmother wand to change yourself into a kid."

"I'd look like a kid, but I'd still be an old lady," said Granny. "This way if something happens, then at least there's someone around who can fight."

"Actually," Daphne said, shoveling half a glowing waffle into her mouth, "I think it's a great idea. He's our age and none of the kids will know who he is."

Sabrina shot her sister a betrayed look, but the little girl didn't see it. She was obviously still angry and refusing to make eye contact with her.

"Oh, no! They won't notice him at all until he turns into a monkey and throws his own poop down the hallway," Sabrina said. "And it's not like the kids aren't going to notice the fifteen layers of crud he has under his pits. He smells like Coney Island after a clam-eating contest."

"Excuse me?" Puck inquired. The boy had slipped into the room without anyone seeing him. Sabrina turned to give him her usual nasty look, but when she saw how he had transformed, she dropped her fork. Puck was clean, shiny, and blond. He'd been scrubbed from head to toe. His leaf-infested, raggedy hair was neat and combed and his teeth sparkled like diamonds. Even his ever-present ratty green hoodie and jeans had been retired and replaced with black cargo pants, a striped baby blue rugby shirt, and brand-new sneakers.

"Puck! You're . . . you're . . ." Sabrina stammered.

"You're a hottie!" Daphne shouted.

Sabrina hated herself, but she had to agree. Puck, the shape-shifter, the royal pain-in-the-rear, had transformed into a cute boy. Sabrina couldn't help but stare, even when he caught her.

"Yes, it's true," he said as he took a seat. "Please, don't hate me because I'm beautiful."

Granny placed a plate of waffles in front of him and he shoved them into his mouth with his bare hands. Whatever spell he had cast on Sabrina quickly faded as she watched him pour some maple syrup down his throat and take a bite out of a stick of butter.

"Puck," Granny Relda groaned as she wiped syrup off the boy's face. "Use a fork. You don't want to have to take another bath, do you?"

"So you ran the garden hose over him. What about the insanity on the inside?" Sabrina asked, still doing her best not to look at him. Puck grinned at her and his big green eyes made her want to cry. She couldn't like Puck! He was disgusting! He wasn't even a real boy!

"Don't worry, old lady," he said with a grin. "I'll behave. Besides, who's going to notice me with these two and their hair?" Suddenly, his head morphed into a donkey's head. He brayed and laughed and spit all over Sabrina.

"Puck, sweetie, no shape-shifting at the table," Granny Relda lectured.

"Just getting it out of my system," the boy said, transforming

back to normal. Sabrina wanted to die. Even when he was being disgusting, he was cute.

Puck looked over at Sabrina, who was wiping his spittle off her face. "Hey ugly, is that your face or did your neck throw up?"

Sabrina was horrified. Did he think she was ugly? Why would he say such a horrible thing in front of everyone? And then it dawned on her—this beautiful boy sitting across from her was still Puck the Trickster. He was the boy who had dumped her in a tub of goo and put a tarantula in her bed. Puck was still Puck, even after a makeover.

"This is ridiculous," she said. "You're sending him because of all this Scarlet Hand message business, when we all know he's the one who did it."

"You think I made all those handprints on the house?" Puck asked.

"Who else?" she cried. "You're the so-called Trickster King. You were pretty mad when Granny sent you to get the Widow. You decided to get your revenge by scaring us. Why not add a little terror to your bag of pranks?"

"I think the glue and buttermilk is seeping out of your hair and into your itty-bitty brain," the boy snapped.

"I believe him," Daphne declared. "He always admits when he does stuff. He's proud of it."

Sabrina turned to her and fumed. Once again, her own sister had taken Puck's side against her.

"Well, I'm pretty proud of my right hook," Sabrina shouted, returning her attention to Puck. "Why don't you come over here and I'll show it to you."

"*Lieblings!*" Granny shouted. The children spun around to face the old woman. Her face was flushed and her little button nose was flaring. "Enough with the shouting!"

"He started it!" Sabrina shouted.

"She started it!" shouted Puck.

"Puck is going to school with you," Granny Relda said firmly. "End of discussion."

Everyone sat silently for a moment, staring down at their breakfasts.

"By the way, marshmallow," Puck said to Daphne, breaking the silence. "How many warts did you find this morning?"

The little girl rolled up her sleeves and showed the boy her arms. "Not one!"

Puck sighed. "That's a shame."

"Why?"

"Well, if you were going to have little ones they would have already shown up. You could put some cream on them and they'd go away in a day or two. But the really big ones take a couple days to show. Those are the kind that end up on the tip of your nose or growing out of your neck. You have to have surgery to get rid of those."

Daphne shrieked and jumped from her seat. In no time she was running up the steps to the bathroom again.

"You better scrub harder this time!" Puck shouted to the little girl.

"How is Captain Maturity going to keep an eye on both of us at the same time?" Sabrina asked. "Daphne and I aren't in the same grade."

"Puck is there to watch you, Sabrina. Daphne will be safe with Snow White," Granny replied. "Snow's a good friend and has volunteered to keep her eye on your sister."

"Don't worry, old lady," Puck crowed. "I'll keep this one out of trouble."

• • •

Granny Relda, Canis, and Puck headed off to meet with Principal Hamelin about enrolling "his majesty" into the sixth grade. As Puck was an Everafter, Granny decided an Everafter should take care of his enrollment and bypassed Mr. Sheepshank entirely. Sabrina was fairly sure the boy was a moron, so she wondered what Granny had planned if the principal decided Puck should be in kindergarten.

Sabrina had assured her grandmother that she could walk to homeroom alone, but regretted the decision when someone grabbed her from behind and dragged her into the girls' restroom. When she spun around, ready to sock her attacker, she found Bella with a brush and some hair spray in hand.

"You need some serious help," the blond girl said, ushering her over to the mirror, turning her around, and going to work on her hair with the brush. "How did you get your hair this way?"

"It's a long story," Sabrina said sheepishly.

Bella tugged and pulled with her brush, coated Sabrina's head with hair spray, and then tied the unruly mane up with a pink rubber band. To Sabrina's surprise, Bella had done something in seconds that Sabrina had been trying to do for herself for two days. She had made Sabrina look normal.

"It'll hold until lunch," Bella said, handing Sabrina her brush and can of hair spray. "After that, well, we may have to call in a professional."

Sabrina was so happy she could have cried. "Thank you."

"Don't thank me," Bella said. "You have the seat in front of mine in science class and with that head of hair there was no way I was going to be able to see the film strip."

Sabrina laughed. It felt good when Bella joined her. Just then, the bell rang.

"We better get to class," the blond girl said. "Old battle-ax will be mad if we're late."

"Didn't you hear?" Sabrina said. "Our teacher was killed last night."

"I think the fumes from the hair spray are affecting your brain. I saw her walking down the hall just a couple of minutes ago."

"Her? Our teacher was a him," Sabrina said.

But Bella had already rushed out of the restroom.

Sabrina walked down the hallway and prepared herself for the sadness and confusion the other students would be feeling when they discovered Mr. Grumpner was dead. She assumed there would be a ceremony to honor their murdered teacher. The school had probably brought in some grief counselors to console them and answer questions. Everyone would make a giant condolence card and sign it for Mr. Grumpner's wife and family. But when she stepped into the classroom, there were no tears running down faces, there were no confused, broken-hearted kids, there was not a single sad face.

In fact, the kids acted as if nothing had happened at all. Like the day before, they were sleepy and bored. Sabrina was shocked. Sure, Mr. Grumpner had been a bitter pill to swallow but he was still a human being and he had died a horrible death. Didn't anyone care?

Bewildered, Sabrina went to her seat, sat down, and scanned the room for anyone who might need someone to talk to. Across the room, Bella smiled and gave her the "thumbs up" gesture.

Has the world gone insane? Sabrina wondered to herself. *A man died in this classroom less than twenty-four hours ago and they're acting like it's just another day!*

A roly-poly woman lumbered into the room and set a handful of books down on Grumpner's desk. She had flaming red hair, done up in a bouffant, and a makeup job that looked as if it had been applied with a paintball gun. Something about her seemed oddly familiar.

"Good morning, class," she said. "Yesterday we were talking about transitive verbs. Let's pass your homework forward and see how you did at identifying them."

Sabrina was dumbfounded. *Homework?*

"Grumpner didn't assign any homework," Sabrina said to the sleepy girl next to her.

"Who's Grumpner?" the girl asked, taking out her assignment and handing it up the aisle.

The teacher glanced around the room, absorbing the faces of

her students. When she spotted Sabrina, her smile suddenly dissolved and was replaced with a bitter scowl. It was then that Sabrina recognized her. Sabrina had seen her when she and Daphne had snuck into the Ferryport Landing Ball—the Queen of Hearts.

"Grimm," she snapped. "A word, please."

Sabrina reluctantly got up from her desk and joined the woman at the front of the room. She had never actually met the queen, but after reading *Alice's Adventures in Wonderland*, Sabrina was familiar with her notorious disciplinary tactics. More than a few citizens of Wonderland had lost their heads when the queen lost her temper. Looking into the woman's face, it seemed to Sabrina that her own head might be next on the chopping block.

"Child, I know what you are up to," the queen said in a low voice.

"I'm not sure what you mean."

"You've come here to spy on me," the woman said. "Well you can tell that old busybody grandmother of yours that she's wasting her time."

"I'm not spying on you," Sabrina said. How dare the woman accuse her of such a thing? The queen didn't even know her.

"I know it drives you Grimms crazy that there are Everafters working around human children."

"I swear I'm not here to spy. I'm eleven. I have to go to school. It's the law," Sabrina snapped. She looked around the room and noticed that even some of the drowsy kids were listening to their conversation. She flushed with anger and embarrassment.

"A likely excuse, but I'm watching you, child. You step out of line just once with me and it's . . ."

"It's what, off with my head?" the girl interrupted as anger flooded over her. She realized she was shouting, but she couldn't help herself. "You're a paranoid old kook. If you want to start off like this on your first day, be my guest!"

"First day?" the queen said nervously. "Sabrina, I've been this class's teacher since the beginning of the year. Don't you remember?"

Suddenly, everything made sense. The reason no one was upset about Grumpner's murder was because no one remembered him. Grumpner had been erased! The Everafters had covered the entire town in forgetful dust and wiped him from everyone's memory. The only reason Sabrina remembered him was because her house was covered with protection spells that kept the family safe from magical attacks.

She didn't know why she was so surprised. The lousy Everafters were always making inconvenient things disappear. When something got in the way, it vanished. Just like her parents. Just like her entire family, if the Everafters got the chance.

"You erased him!" Sabrina shouted, unable to control her anger. "You wiped him away, just like that! Just like you did with my parents, but I won't let you do it again. You tell your dirty Everafter friends that I'm going to find my mom and dad. And I'm going to find who killed Mr. Grumpner, too!"

The queen's face reeled in horror. Sabrina had betrayed an unspoken rule of Ferryport Landing—never reveal the truth! She looked up at the nasty teacher's face, hoping the queen could see that she was tired of secrets. Daphne was right. Mr. Grumpner's murder needed to be solved, if only to show the Everafters that they couldn't get away with their tricks anymore.

Suddenly, Wendell, the boy who had been late for school the day before, rushed into the room. He looked confused for a moment as he spotted the queen, then he recovered and hurried down the aisle to his seat, an odd, chalky dust trailing behind him. He sat down awkwardly and hid his face in his textbook.

Sabrina's eyes watered and she sneezed loudly as the cloud of dust settled to the floor.

"Cut it out, Grimm," Toby cried from across the room. "You're spraying your cooties all over the place."

Sabrina turned on the boy, walked down the aisle, and grabbed him by the shirt collar. Still full of rage, she shouted, "Shut your mouth you little bug-eyed freak!"

Toby stared into her face and just smiled.

"Mrs. Heart, I'm sorry to interrupt," a voice said from the doorway. Sabrina spun around and saw Principal Hamelin. "I'd like to introduce a new student."

"Take your seat, Ms. Grimm," the queen said between gritted teeth. The angry girl marched back to her desk.

"Mrs. Heart, class, this is Robin Goodfellow," the principal said as Puck marched into the room, waving and bowing as if he were a movie star.

"*Taa-daa,*" Puck sang. "Please, don't make a fuss."

"Robin is here all the way from Akron, Ohio, and he'll be staying with Sabrina Grimm's family," Hamelin announced.

"Robin Goodfellow?" the queen muttered knowingly. It was obvious to Sabrina that the teacher recognized the boy.

Puck winked at her. "That's my name, don't wear it out," he crowed.

"Take a seat in the back. There's one near your friend."

The boy looked around the room. "Is that the only seat available? The Grimm girl tends to have a very foul odor," he said with a wicked grin. "She's a real stinker."

The half of the class that wasn't asleep roared with laughter and Sabrina blushed.

"And she's got quite a temper, too," the queen replied. "Sorry, Mr. Goodfellow. If the rest of the class has to suffer, so do you."

The students roared again.

"So, Mrs. Heart, he's all yours," the principal said and left the room.

Sabrina's head was pounding and she had a fever. How had she gotten so angry so quickly? Mirror was right. Puberty was really screwing with her head and if she didn't get control over it she was going to be the school weirdo forever. She glanced around the room and noticed that kids were staring at her. How humiliating the whole thing had been. The only kids who didn't seem to care were the ones who had slept through it all and Wendell. The chubby little Everafter boy had been busy reading and keeping his head down the whole time Puck was being introduced by the principal, almost as if he'd wanted to avoid his father's gaze. There was something unusual about the boy. His feet were covered in white chalk. It had made Sabrina sneeze, just like the dust they had found in Mr. Grumpner's footprints. This odd boy with the runny nose had been in the same place their murdered teacher had been.

"Ms. Grimm," Mrs. Heart said—she had come down the

aisle and was standing over Sabrina with her grade book in hand—"No homework today?"

Sabrina's eyes flared as they met the queen's. "I didn't know we had any homework today," she snapped.

"That's a shame, Ms. Grimm," the teacher said with a wicked smile. "I'm going to have to give you a zero."

The girl met her grin with a bitter scowl.

"Since you're having trouble keeping up with your assignments, maybe we should set up some special time for you to get them done," Mrs. Heart said. "I'll see you in detention this afternoon."

"What's a detention?" Puck asked.

"It means I have to stay after school for an hour," Sabrina whispered

"An hour!" The boy laughed. "That's the most twisted, depraved punishment I have ever heard of. I've been here for five minutes and it's already an intolerable agony!"

"Well, then, *Mr. Goodfellow,* maybe you should join her," Mrs. Heart suggested.

"Your Majesty!" Puck cried, leaping from his seat. He threw his arms around the woman and wailed. "Show some mercy!"

The Queen of Hearts waited patiently for Puck's dramatics to end and for the students to stop giggling. When he released her, the teacher spun around and headed to the front of the classroom.

"Now, class, let's talk about past participles," she said, turning toward the chalkboard. On the queen's back was a sheet of paper that read I KISS GOATS. The kids who were awake fell over themselves laughing.

The teacher spun around and flashed the class a mascara-heavy evil eye. She turned back to the board and the class exploded again.

"Anyone who wants to join Ms. Grimm and Mr. Goodfellow tonight in detention, just keep it up," she shouted.

By the time the bell rang, the entire class was looking at Puck as if he were a rock star.

"Hilarious!" one kid snorted as the students emptied into the hall. Puck absorbed their praise like a greedy sponge and agreed with each one wholeheartedly that he was indeed a genius. But Sabrina had no interest in Puck's groupies. Her eyes were fixed on Wendell, who now hurried down the hallway, followed by a cloud of dust. She rushed after him.

"Hey, stink-pot," Puck said, breaking away from his followers. "You're not supposed to leave my sight."

Sabrina didn't reply. Instead, she darted through crowds and dodged open lockers as she trailed the chubby boy through the over-packed hallway. He raced down a flight of stairs and slipped through a door. By the time Sabrina caught up, he had already slammed the door behind him. The sign on it read BOILER ROOM.

"Where are you going?" Puck asked, grabbing Sabrina's wrist and pulling her back before she could open the door.

"I think that boy knows something about Grumpner's death," she replied, reaching for the door.

"You're not supposed to go anywhere without me."

"Well, you're here now, let's go."

"I don't feel like it."

"Puck, it's the boiler room. I bet it's dirty and gross in there," Sabrina said, trying to play to the boy's biggest weakness—filth. "I bet there's a greasy floor you could roll around on."

Puck's eyes lit up and he nodded vigorously. It was nice to see that she could manipulate him when it was important. She reached for the doorknob again, but before she could turn it, a muscular, grizzled-looking man stepped in her way.

"Where do you kids think you're going?" he asked. He was tall and strong, with arms as big as tree trunks and a chest as wide as the family car. It was obvious that he hadn't shaved in several days and could probably use some sleep. His blue coverall uniform had a patch on it that told everyone his name was Charlie and the smell coming off of him told everyone his uniform needed a trip to the laundromat. But it was the mop slung over his shoulder that told her this was the school janitor, and the boiler room was his domain.

"I was looking for my next class," Sabrina lied.

"In the boiler room?" Charlie laughed, spraying his cornedbeef-and-cigarette breath all over her. "Ain't nothing in there but a bunch of mops and brooms."

"My mistake," she said. She turned around and together she and Puck headed down the hallway. She snuck a peek back, hoping Charlie had moved on, but he was still there, leaning against the door.

"I could lure him upstairs and push him out a window," Puck offered.

"No, we can't do that. We'll come back later. For now, just go to your next class," Sabrina replied. "Where is it?"

She snatched his schedule out of his hand and looked at it. "Puck, you're in all my classes!"

"The old lady and Canis negotiated it with the principal," the boy explained.

Sabrina knew what kind of negotiating Mr. Canis could do. Now Sabrina would have Puck practically riding on her back.

There were several kids walking behind them and one of them laughed loudly and said, "Hello, Smelly Stink-pot."

Sabrina spun around to see who had insulted her but the kids just walked away.

"Smelly Stink-pot? What does that mean?" Sabrina asked Puck.

"Who knows?" he said. "Kids can be cruel."

It would be hours before Bella stopped her in the hallway and removed a sign that had been taped onto Sabrina's back. It read, PLEASED TO MEET YOU, I'M SMELLY STINK-POT!

• • •

The rest of the day, Sabrina and Puck kept a watchful eye out for Wendell, but it seemed as if the boy had disappeared. During a break between classes, Puck even rushed outside and summoned some pixies with his flute, to look for their chubby suspect. As Sabrina and Puck waited for word back, they went from one class to the next, and in each the Trickster King did his best to humiliate his housemate. Unlike a normal kid, Puck didn't bring pencils or a notebook to class; he brought what he called the essentials: a squirt gun, stink pellets, a shock buzzer, and his personal favorite—a whoopee cushion. Now, to Sabrina, fart jokes were so old-fashioned. She believed kids were pretty sophisticated in the twenty-first century. It would take more than an obnoxious noise to get a modern kid laughing.

Unfortunately, Sabrina was wrong. Puck let the whoopee cushion go in every class, making it seem as if Sabrina were having intestinal issues, and the kids just thought it got funnier and funnier. Eventually, he added a little acting to his routine, pretending to gag on Sabrina's imaginary fumes. When this proved to be wildly popular as well, it quickly evolved into an elaborate death scene, which ended with Puck shaking in convulsions on the floor. His performances, and Sabrina's threats of a serious beating, helped the two rack up an impressive five detentions apiece by midday. At the rate they were going, Sabrina suspected they would be in detention until they were twenty-five.

So, as they headed for gym class, she smiled, knowing revenge was within her grasp. Puck was about to get what he had coming to him.

"OK class," Ms. Spangler said as she tossed a ball back and forth between her hands. "We've got a new student today. His name is Robin and he says he's never actually played dodgeball."

Even from across the room, Sabrina could see Toby's and Natalie's eyes light up with excitement. Bella, who was standing nearby, leaned over to her. "Your friend is in serious trouble."

Puck waved to everyone, unaware that attention was the last

thing he wanted in this class. Once everyone got an eyeful of him, Ms. Spangler divided the class into two teams. Puck and Sabrina found themselves standing next to each other.

"How do you play this game?" he asked.

"People throw balls at you," she said. "If they hit you, then you're out."

"Let me get this straight. The object of this game is to hit someone with a ball. Can you hit them in the head?"

Sabrina nodded, eyeing the opposing team to avoid a sneak attack.

"And you can hit them as hard as you want?"

"That's actually encouraged. But be careful—if they catch it you're out."

"Does anyone ever catch the ball?"

"Rarely."

"How diabolical!" Puck cried. "It's so twisted, it's brilliant! Are you any good at this 'dodgeball'?"

"I used to be," Sabrina grumbled, staring at the two children directly across from her on the other team, Toby and the big goon Natalie, who were staring back at her with evil grins on their faces. They were like vultures, waiting to take a bite of her.

Ms. Spangler blew her whistle and the insanity began.

A ball whizzed past Sabrina's head and smacked into Bella.

Sabrina was surprised. The day before, the girl had been so agile, but now it seemed like Bella had actually stepped into the ball, as if she wanted to be knocked out of the game.

The blond girl shrugged her shoulders. "Good luck," she said to Sabrina, as she made her way over to the sidelines. Sabrina looked up to see Toby and Natalie. Both were grinning. Toby winged his ball straight at her head and just before it smashed her in the nose, Puck reached over and caught it.

"Toby's out!" Ms. Spangler shouted. Dejected, the boy scowled and sulked over to the sidelines.

"Now what do I do with it?" Puck asked.

"Throw it at somebody," Sabrina said impatiently.

Puck wound up, ready to smack Sabrina right in the face with the ball.

"Not me, you idiot!" she cried, pointing at the opposite team. "Them!"

Puck threw his ball at a red-haired boy standing close to the front. It rocketed across the room like a missile, hit the red-headed kid in the chest, and sent him flying backward ten yards. The class stopped playing and let out a collective gasp.

"Kevin is out!" Ms. Spangler said, unsympathetic to the boy's obvious injuries.

Every kid looked at Puck as if he had just suggested adding

another day to the school week. Even kids on his team seemed afraid of him, and when the game resumed, Puck was public enemy number one.

Balls came from every direction and the boy managed to duck, jump, and somersault around every one. He bent in impossible directions that no normal human being ever could. He stood on his hands and let balls fly between his feet. He taunted everyone, which only made them want to smash him in the face even more, but every effort failed. When the already sleepy kids were thoroughly exhausted, Puck began to collect their weak tosses. In no time he had collected almost every ball and had laid them at his feet. When the kids realized what he had done, they whimpered. Even Natalie let out a little cry.

Puck picked up the first of his collection and winged it at a boy standing nearby. The ball hit the kid so hard he slid across the floor and out the gym doors. Puck picked up another ball, and another, and another, tossing them at impossible speeds. A tall skinny girl was hit so hard her shoes flew off her feet. One ball hit a group of kids, bouncing off of one and then hitting the next and the next, until they all tipped over like bowling pins. Even Ms. Spangler got cracked hard in the back and nearly swallowed her whistle. By the time it was over, Sabrina, Puck, and Natalie were the only ones left standing.

"No boundaries!" Ms. Spangler said.

"What's that mean?" Puck asked.

"It means we can go after her," Sabrina said, pointing at Natalie.

He clapped his hands like a happy baby. "School is awesome!" he shouted. He picked up a ball and handed it to Sabrina.

Sabrina was so happy she could have kissed Puck. Quickly shaking off this thought, she helped him stalk the big girl around the gym. Natalie huffed like an angry bull.

"If you know what's good for you, you'll drop those balls right now," she threatened them.

"You're probably right," Sabrina said, tossing the ball at the girl as hard as she could. It smashed into the side of Natalie's face and she fell down. Sabrina had knocked the bully down for the second time in two days.

"Natalie is out!" Ms. Spangler shouted. "No sides!"

Sabrina turned to congratulate Puck, just as a ball crashed into the side of her face and sent her reeling. The class cheered and Puck raised his hand in triumph.

"I won!" he cried. He raised both arms into the air and ran around the gym shouting, "Victory lap!"

Sabrina could already feel her lip swelling.

• • •

By the time lunch rolled around, Sabrina was ready to strangle the boy. So when she saw Daphne's smiling face in the cafeteria, it was like seeing a rainbow. The little girl was surrounded by her classmates, who, as they had the day before, looked at her as if she were a movie star. When Daphne spotted Sabrina and Puck, she excused herself and joined them at a table in the far corner of the room.

"How has your day been?" she asked.

"It's been horrible," Sabrina said.

"Tell my sister I wasn't talking to her," Daphne said to Puck. "I was talking to you."

Sabrina rolled her eyes. "How long are you going to be mad at me?"

"Remind my sister that I just said I was not talking to her," the little girl said to Puck.

Puck grinned. "The squirt says she isn't talking to you."

"Get over it!" Sabrina cried.

"Tell my sister when she stops being a snot I will get over it."

"She says when you stop being a disgusting booger-crusted freak she will honor you with a conversation, but until then, shove off," Puck said.

"This is ridiculous," the older girl said, staring down at her serving of not-too-green green beans.

"Ask my sister what *ridiculous* means," Daphne said.

"She wants to know what . . ."

"I heard her!" Sabrina growled at the boy. "It means you are being silly! It means you are being a baby!"

"Tell my sister that I'm rubber and she's glue and whatever she says bounces off me and sticks to her."

"Your sister says . . ."

"Puck!" Sabrina shouted. She turned back to her food and took a bite of something she thought might be chicken. It wasn't even close.

"Well, if you're not going to talk to me, then you won't know that I've found a clue," she said.

Daphne's face lit up as bright as the sun. "What kind of clue?"

"Are you done with the silent treatment?" her sister asked.

"Depends on how good the clue is."

"You know those dusty footprints we were following last night? Well there's a kid in my homeroom whose feet were covered in the same dust."

"What did you do?" Daphne asked, interested despite herself.

"I tried to follow him, but he slipped into the boiler room," Sabrina said. "We're going to have to come back after everyone's gone and do some snooping."

Daphne smiled and hugged Sabrina.

Puck sniffed the creamed corn on his tray. He reached down with his bare hand and scooped some up. Then he licked it with his tongue. "Any of those disgusting warts show up, yet?"

"Ms. White told me that you don't get warts from touching frogs," the little girl growled. "Not even frog-girls."

"Ahh, I'm sorry to see that little joke die." The boy sighed as creamed corn dripped down his wrist and onto his clean shirt. "I had you completely freaked out."

"Hardy-har-har, Puck, you are so un-punk rock," Daphne said, turning her attention to her sister. "So, what's the plan?"

"First, you have to get a detention," Sabrina said as she eyed her gray hamburger.

"What?" Daphne cried.

"Puck got us in trouble, so we have to stay after school. Since the two of us have to stay, you might as well get in trouble, too. We should try to stick together."

"How am I supposed to get a detention?" the little girl asked.

"I don't know! Insult your teacher or something."

"I can't do that to Ms. White!"

"Yes you can. Be annoying!" Sabrina suggested. "You do it to me every day."

Daphne looked as if she was going to cry.

• • •

When the children met at the end of the last period, Daphne was back to giving Sabrina the silent treatment. Sabrina asked her how she'd managed to get detention, but she wouldn't answer. Sabrina shrugged. If she worried every time her sister got mad at her, she'd never have time to do anything else. Daphne would get over it. The important thing was that they were all together. Nothing bad could happen when they were together.

They walked down the hallway toward the detention room and Puck was nothing but complaints.

"I can't believe I have to be subjected to this torture," he whined. "I am royalty. To say anything I do is inappropriate in school is just foolish. Everything I do is majestic and regal."

"So when you were picking your nose in Mr. Cafferty's class, that was regal?" Sabrina asked.

"Absolutely," he said. "Back home people stand out in the freezing rain for days just to hear a rumor that I picked my nose."

"Ugh," was all Sabrina could say to Puck's disgusting conversation.

"This detention is going to be horrible. I've heard stories. Some kids go into that class and never come out, and the ones that do aren't the same."

"Aren't you being a little dramatic?"

"Not at all," Puck insisted. "From what I hear, this detention is a house of horrors."

Sabrina rolled her eyes and opened the detention room door. Immediately she put her hand over Daphne's eyes. Mrs. Heart lay in one corner of the room. Snow White struggled to her feet in another, and in the center was a skeleton in shredded coveralls with a name patch still visible—Charlie. The killer had left one identifying mark on the fabric of the coveralls—a bright red handprint.

"See, I told you!" Puck said proudly.

"It's gross, isn't it?" Daphne asked, turning into her sister's arms and hiding her face in Sabrina's sweater.

"Yes, it's gross," Sabrina whispered.

"I guess this means we don't have detention," Puck said.

Daphne pulled herself away from her sister and rushed to Ms. White. The teacher didn't look seriously injured, but was dizzy and disoriented. The children helped her to her feet and sat her at one of the desks in the classroom. Sabrina kneeled down to check on Mrs. Heart. She was breathing normally, but was out cold.

"What happened, Ms. White?" Sabrina asked.

The teacher looked confused and mumbled, but only one word was distinguishable: "Wendell."

Suddenly, there was a loud thump outside the window, followed by a painful moan. The children ran to the window and Sabrina stuck her head out. Below her was Wendell. The boy had jumped out the window, tumbled end over end, and was climbing to his feet.

"Hey!" she shouted. The boy looked up and his face went pale. He darted off toward the woods as fast as his chubby little legs could carry him.

Puck's enormous wings burst out of his back. "I'll get the little piggy."

Sabrina grabbed his arm before he could fly away. "Someone might see you," she cried, dragging the boy back from the window. Instead, she crawled out herself, dropping five feet before landing safely on the ground. Daphne followed and her sister caught her. Puck refused Sabrina's assistance and jumped on his own, his wings no longer visible.

"He's headed for the forest," Sabrina shouted and the three children sprinted across the field. Wendell was not a fast runner, but he had a big head start. He had already disappeared into the forest by the time the children reached the tree line.

"We lost him," Sabrina groaned.

"No, he left a trail," Puck said, pointing at deep, muddy footprints. The group raced on, following the trail.

"He's confused," the boy said as they followed the footprints up a hill. "He goes in one direction and then turns back and runs the other way. It's slowing him down. We'll find him soon."

Puck was right. It wasn't long before they found the chubby boy, cornered against a steep rocky wall. When Wendell saw them, he whimpered like a dog and looked frantically for an escape.

"It's not what you think," he said, wiping his nose with his handkerchief.

"Then why are you running?" Sabrina asked.

"I was trying to help," he cried. "I'm trying to stop them."

"Who's them?" Daphne asked.

Suddenly, the frightened boy pulled out a small harmonica and raised it to his lips.

"Don't make me use this!" he shouted.

"C'mon, tubby," Puck said. "We know you're the killer. We'll take you back and call the cops. It'll all be over in no time. Don't worry, I hear the electric chair only hurts for a second."

Wendell blew a long, sour note into his harmonica and the whole forest erupted with chatter and scurrying. The noise grew louder and louder and Sabrina thought that at any moment some horrible monster or giant was going to charge out of the brush. But the noise stopped suddenly, and a furry little bunny hopped out from behind a tree. It was the cutest brown rabbit she had ever seen and it bounded over to them and stopped at their feet. It looked up at the children with its soft, warm eyes and made a little twittering noise.

"A bunny!" Daphne cried, as she knelt down to pet it. "I love him!"

The rabbit snapped at her finger and let out a horrible, angry hiss.

"An evil bunny," the little girl said, yanking her finger away.

"So that's what your harmonica does?" Puck laughed. "Sends a rabbit to kill us?"

Wendell didn't say anything. He didn't have to. His silence was filled by the sound of hundreds of rabbits pouring into the clearing as if they had heard Puck's taunt. They jostled one another for room, then turned and faced Wendell as if he was some kind of general. It was obvious the boy was controlling them.

"Guys, I forgot to tell you the other clue I discovered," Sabrina said nervously. "Wendell is an Everafter. He's the Pied Piper's son and apparently the magic runs in the family."

"Now you listen to me," Puck said, as his wings sprouted from his back and flapped vigorously, until he was floating above the ground. "You're a killer and from what I've been told, that's against the law these days. Now, we can do this the easy way or we can do it the hard way."

"Puck, shut up," Sabrina demanded, but the Trickster just kept on talking and Wendell's face grew more and more desperate. Each furry little rodent twitched with eagerness, waiting for the boy to give a command.

"If you think a bunch of hairy little garden thieves are going to stop me, you are sadly mistaken," Puck continued. "So, call off your fur balls or I'm going to skin the lot of them and make me the biggest winter coat you've ever seen!"

Wendell lifted his harmonica to his mouth and another sour note rang through the air. The rabbits instantly turned and faced the kids. Their soft brown eyes were now red with anger.

"Get them," Wendell shouted and, like a furry army, the first wave of rabbits lunged at the children.

7

That's the best you can do, fat boy?" Puck shouted, spinning on his heels and transforming into a massive thirteen-foot brown bear. He roared so viciously that Sabrina felt it in her toes, but it did nothing to stop the rabbits. They dove onto Puck in waves, knocking his mammoth body to the ground and covering him from head to toe.

"Puck!" the girls shouted, terrified that he'd been killed. And for a brief moment it seemed as if their fears were true. But the boy soared out of the bunny pile, giant wings flapping, and into the sky. He dipped back down, snatched each girl by the hand, and began an awkward effort to fly out of the forest.

"Next time, why doesn't one of you tell me to shut up?" Puck cried.

Daphne and Sabrina looked at each other incredulously.

"I am so going to have nightmares about this," Daphne whined.

Puck sailed through the forest, barely managing to avoid the giant cedars and fir trees that seemed to appear out of nowhere. He ducked between branches and flapped fiercely to raise the girls over the brush and pricker bushes on the forest floor. One desperate effort to dodge a huge Chinese maple tree forced him to dive close to the ground, where one of the rabbits leaped up and sank its teeth into Sabrina's pant leg. She shook it off and it disappeared into the furry sea below.

"Head for the river," Sabrina cried. "They can't follow us over the water."

Puck frowned at her. "I know what I'm doing," he growled.

"If you knew what you were doing, we wouldn't have two million zombie bunnies chasing us!" she shouted.

"Guys," Daphne said, trying to get their attention, but her sister was too angry to listen.

"How was I supposed to know that kid was mentally unhinged?" Puck said.

"I don't know," Sabrina snapped. "Maybe when we found him running from a dead body?"

"Guys!" Daphne shouted.

"What!" Puck and Sabrina snapped.

"LOOK OUT!"

Sabrina looked up to see a fifteen-foot-high fence in front of them. Puck made a desperate swerve and narrowly missed smashing into it, but the near collision didn't slow down the argument.

"I don't know why I'm involved in this, anyway!" he cried. "I'm one of the bad guys!"

"The only bad thing about you is your breath!" Sabrina shouted. "All we ever hear about is Puck the villain! What kind of villain has creamed corn all over his shirt?"

The boy snarled, made a dramatic turn to the left, and looked Sabrina dead in the eye.

"You want to see how bad I can be?" he growled. "I'll show you what I'm capable of!"

He soared into the backyard of someone's home, a stocky senior citizen who was puttering around his yard. As the trio flew past him they heard the man shout, "Agnes! The rabbits have been digging up the yard, again. I swear, the next one I see is going to wish it hadn't been born!"

Puck howled with laughter as he led the bunnies right through the poor man's yard. By the time the old fellow saw them coming, it was too late. Sabrina caught a glimpse of his shocked face as the first wave of rabbits knocked him to the ground. "Agnes!" he cried. They hopped over him as if he wasn't even there.

"That was mean!" Daphne shouted at Puck.

Flapping vigorously, the boy flew across the street just as an old woman's car came to a stop at the intersection. She was a tiny old lady who could barely see over the dashboard. She must have been legally blind, too, because she waited patiently, unblinking, for Puck and the two girls to fly across the road, followed by a couple thousand rabbits. When her way was clear, she drove off as if nothing unusual had happened at all.

"People are going to see us! You've got to get us off the street," Sabrina insisted.

"Oh, you want me to get us off the street? Fine, your wish is my command," Puck yelled. He flew straight toward a house where a tall man had just opened his front door. As the man bent over to pick up his newspaper, Puck flew inside.

"No! Don't," Daphne cried as Puck sailed through the living room, into the dining room, and flapped awkwardly over the table. Below them, two small children were setting the table, oblivious to the scene above their heads. They were hungrily eyeing a glistening golden ham in the center of a dinner feast. Puck dipped lower and Daphne accidentally kicked the ham and a bowl of mashed potatoes onto the floor. The family's two hyperactive English springer spaniels then raced into the room and tore into the fallen food.

"Chelsea! Maxine! No!" the mother shouted, running in from

the kitchen and desperately trying to drag the remains of the ham from their greedy mouths. "Bad dogs!" She didn't look up, but the children did.

"So sorry," Daphne shouted to the open-mouthed children as Puck flew into the kitchen. They found the back door. Sabrina opened it and they zipped outside. The rabbits had noticed their detour and now tumbled through the house, knocking over furniture and sending lamps crashing to the floor. They blasted out of windows and knocked the back door off its hinges and still managed to gain ground.

Sabrina looked up at Puck and saw the proud grin on his face.

"That wasn't funny," she snapped.

"Yes it was," he said.

"They're still coming," Daphne cried. "We have to go somewhere they can't go."

"We're on our way," Puck crowed. Soon they were out of the neighborhoods and flying back over acres of overgrown woods. In no time, the Hudson River stretched out before them.

"If we fly out over the river, they won't be able to follow," Sabrina said.

"Oh, we're going over the river all right, but not to save you from the rabbits," Puck cried. "We're going over because you questioned my villainy."

Sabrina looked up into his face. "You wouldn't dare!"

"That's another thing you shouldn't question!"

He flapped his wings hard and soon the three were soaring over the rocky cliffs, high above the Hudson. Sabrina watched as the rabbits raced to the cliff's edge and then abruptly stopped.

"Anyone ready for a swim?" Puck asked.

"Don't do it!" Sabrina demanded.

"Next time you talk to me, maybe you'll do well to remember that I am royalty."

But before Puck could dump them into the icy water, his body buckled as if he had flown into a brick wall. Sabrina lost her grip on him and dropped like a stone, landing hard in the freezing river below. She sank deep into the river then swam frantically to reach the surface in time to see Daphne splash down beside her.

"Daphne!" she screamed as her sister sank below the surface. Sabrina dived into the water and, after several moments of frantic searching, her already numb fingers found something soft and fluffy. It was Daphne! Sabrina wrapped her arms around her sister and pulled her to the surface.

The little girl gasped for air and started choking as a mouthful of water spilled from her lips.

"Where's Puck?" she asked, between painful coughs.

Sabrina scanned the waves nearby, but there was no sign of the boy.

"Puck!" she shouted. There was no response.

Sabrina turned her sister toward the shore. "Can you make it?" she asked.

Daphne nodded. Sabrina let her go and the little girl doggy-paddled toward land. Luckily, their father had taught them both how to swim at the YMCA near their apartment and Daphne had taken to it like a fish. She'd be fine.

"Puck!" Sabrina shouted again. She took a deep breath and dived back into the cold water, knowing she didn't have a lot of time. The water was so icy she was losing feeling in her feet. She moved back and forth, searching in the dark waters with her hands, but finding nothing. Finally, her lungs ached for oxygen, and she was forced to return to the surface.

Gasping for breath, she noticed something odd floating in the distance. When she looked closer she knew what it was—giant, glittery wings. She swam as hard as she could and found Puck facedown in the water. She turned him over. His face was blue. She wrapped her arm around his cold body and swam to shore as best she could. There, Daphne helped her drag the motion-less boy onto dry ground.

"Please don't be dead, Puck!" the little girl cried.

"Stand back," Sabrina said. She tilted the boy's head and looked in his mouth for obstructions. She had taken life-saving lessons in school but had only tried CPR once on a rubber dummy—never on a real, live person! Worse, she remembered her teacher had given her a C-minus for the course.

She took a deep breath and placed her mouth on Puck's, blowing all the air she could down his windpipe. Nothing happened. She did it again. She remembered to press on his sternum to force air in and out of his lungs. She counted off fifteen compressions and then returned to blowing into his mouth.

Suddenly, his eyes opened and he shoved Sabrina away.

"I'm contaminated!" he cried, wiping his mouth.

"Puck, you're alive!" Daphne shouted and hugged the boy.

"Of course I'm alive," the boy said, crawling to his feet. His wings disappeared into his back. "I happen to be immortal."

"We thought . . . you were . . . I tried," Sabrina stammered.

"You thought you'd give me a kiss while I was vulnerable," Puck said indignantly. "I guess I'm going to have to stop taking baths if you can't keep your hands to yourself."

Sabrina was so angry she was sure steam was coming out of her ears.

"What happened to you?" Daphne asked.

"I forgot how close the old witch's barrier was. I slammed into it pretty hard." Puck laughed.

"You think this is funny?" Sabrina snapped. "We could have died out there."

"Children?" a soft voice called out from behind them. They spun around and found Ms. White standing on the banks of the river. "We need to get you out of this cold."

• • •

"Well, I knew something was strange. I'd never had a student ask me for a detention before," the pretty teacher said, winking at Daphne, who sat in the front seat of the car with her. Puck and Sabrina huddled in the backseat under a blanket.

"Knowing your father as I did, I figured the two of you were up to something, so I thought I'd better come down to the detention room and find out what was going on. When I got there, the Queen of Hearts was trying to fight off the monster with a chair," she continued.

The children were stunned.

"Monster!" they said in unison.

"Was it a giant spider or a frog-girl?" Sabrina asked.

"Neither!" Snow White replied. "This was more like a wolf or a Bigfoot. I think it ate Charlie. It was going after the queen next, but lucky for her, I arrived. I managed to distract it, but I knew I couldn't fight it by myself."

"What did you do?" said Daphne.

"Nothing. I didn't have to. Wendell saved us," the teacher continued. "He blew into his harmonica and it seemed to stop the monster, at least for a second, but then it jumped out the window and ran off. Wendell was chasing after it when you saw him. I suppose if he were older he could have stopped the thing all together. His dad has been known to halt elephants in their tracks."

"So Wendell can control things with his harmonica," Sabrina said, her voice full of suspicion. "Just like his father, the Pied Piper. How do you know he was trying to save you? Maybe he was trying to help that thing escape."

"Oh, no!" Snow White argued. "That sweet little boy had nothing to do with this."

"Ms. White, when we confronted him, he sent an army of rabbits after us," Sabrina said. "Besides, he's an Everafter."

"What's that supposed to mean?" the teacher said.

"It means he has secrets," Sabrina said. "All of you walk around here, hiding behind your magic and when something bad happens, you just make it disappear. *Poof,* and the problem is gone!"

"Sabrina, shut up!" Daphne cried.

"I'm not hiding, young lady," Ms. White replied coolly, as she pulled her car into Granny's driveway. "Everafters are not all alike."

Before Sabrina could argue, Granny Relda and Elvis came running out to meet them.

"*Lieblings*, where have you been?" their grandmother said, rushing down the driveway as the children climbed out of the car. Elvis was so excited to see Daphne, he accidentally knocked her down with a series of excited kisses.

"In the river," the little girl said. "It was fun but very cold."

"In the river?" Granny Relda asked. "Why were you in the river?"

"The rabbits chased us there," Daphne replied matter-of-factly.

The old woman threw her hands into the air. "What are you talking about?"

"They've had quite an afternoon, Relda," Ms. White said as she got out of her car. "They could use some warm clothes and some soup."

"Thank you for bringing them home, Snow," the old woman said, taking the teacher's hand.

"My pleasure," Snow White said. She turned and went back to her car, but then, suddenly, she turned and eyed Sabrina. "I hope you'll think about what I said. You can't judge the many by the actions of the few."

Granny raised a curious eyebrow at Sabrina as the teacher drove away.

"*Lieblings*, we have to get you into the bath," the old woman said. "Daphne, you go first, and make that water good and warm."

Daphne nodded and rushed into the house, with Elvis at her heels.

"I think I'll go up to my room," Puck said, spinning around and heading for the stairs.

"Absolutely not!" Granny Relda commanded. "You're next in the bathtub."

The boy's face tightened as if he had just bitten into a lemon. "I've already had all the baths I'm ever going to take. We're not going to make this a habit. I have a reputation. I'm a master villain. What will people say if they hear an old lady is forcing me into the bathtub every ten minutes?" he demanded. "I'll be the laughingstock of every tree gnome, pixie, hobgoblin, and brownie from here to Wonderland."

"Well, everyone is just going to have to think a little less of you then, Mr. Master Villain," Granny said. "Now, rush upstairs and change out of those clothes and don't put on that ratty green sweatshirt and jeans. Put on something clean!"

Puck pouted, but Granny Relda didn't budge. After several moments of staring her down, he spun around and stomped into the house.

"You, too," the old woman said to Sabrina. "Run upstairs and put on a bathrobe and some warm socks and come back down. I could use your help with the soup."

The old "I need your help" routine, the girl thought as she plodded up the steps to change out of her dripping clothes. Nine times out of ten, when an adult asked a child for help with something, it meant they were planning a lecture. But Sabrina thought it best just to change and get it over with. Once she was out of her clothes and into a warm robe, she headed back downstairs, passing the bathroom door, where she could hear Daphne begging Elvis to get into the tub with her. A tremendous splash told Sabrina that the little girl had gotten her wish.

When she passed Puck's room, she heard a horrible smashing sound inside. Apparently, the idea of another bath was not sitting well with the Trickster King. She wondered what his garden paradise would look like after the fairy prince got through with his temper tantrum.

"Sabrina? Is that you, *liebling*?" Granny called from the kitchen.

The girl followed the voice and found the old woman had already put a pot of broth on the stove and was chopping carrots and celery into little pieces on a cutting board.

"What are we making?" Sabrina asked sarcastically. "Kangaroo-tail soup? Cream of fungus?"

"Chicken noodle," Granny replied. "Why don't you have a seat on that stool? I think it's time you and I had a talk."

Sabrina rolled her eyes, but sat down.

"You've got a lot of anger in you, child," said Granny Relda.

Sure she was angry! Who wouldn't be? She was tired of the secrets and the lies. Tired of the things hidden underneath, tired of the surprises that popped up every single day. No one in this town was what they seemed. One of them had her parents. Was she supposed to walk around making friends and passing out cookies?

"I get angry, too," her grandmother continued. "My son and daughter-in-law are out there somewhere and I can't find them. Every night, after you girls are asleep, I ask Mirror to let me take a look at them. In a way, it makes me happy that they are still there, sleeping so peacefully, not even knowing all the trouble that we're going through to find them.

"And I crawl back in bed and I want to scream," Granny said, tossing the chopped celery into the big silver pot. "I hate feeling helpless and I blame myself for not being able to find them. After all, there's more magic and books in this house than in ten thousand fairy tales combined, and yet I'm no closer to bringing them home today than I was six months ago.

"Sometimes I look around this town and wonder if the person responsible for all of our heartache is sitting next to me in the coffee shop," she continued. "Or maybe it's the lady behind me in line at the supermarket or the woman who styles my hair at the beauty parlor. Maybe it's the nice man at the filling station who pumps gas into the car. Maybe it's the paperboy or the mailman or that girl who sells cookies for the scouts."

Sabrina's heart began to rise. Granny Relda felt exactly the way she did. Why hadn't she told them her true feelings about the town? It would have kept Sabrina from feeling so guilty and confused about the place.

"You're looking at the wrong people," she said, feeling encouraged by the old woman's revelation. "You should be looking at the Everafters."

"*Liebling*, Everafters are people." Granny said, setting down her knife. "They have families and homes and dreams."

"And murderous plots, kidnapping schemes, and plans to destroy the town."

"You don't really believe they are all bad, do you? What about Snow White and the sheriff?"

"They're Everafters. We just haven't discovered what they're really up to yet."

"*Sabrina!*" Granny Relda shouted. "No grandchild of mine is going to be a bigot! Hatred can grow, child, into something terrible and beyond your control!"

"You're defending the Everafters? They took my parents away and you are defending them?" Sabrina cried. She jumped off the stool.

"Yes, I'm going to defend them and anyone else who people choose to discriminate against."

"How can you do it?" Sabrina screamed, on the verge of tears.

"Because that is what I choose to do," the old woman said. "Yes, there are bad people among the Everafters but there are bad people among us all. You can't blame them all for the actions of one. I know it is difficult when you don't know who is responsible, but the guilt cannot be everyone's."

Sabrina felt as if she were being suffocated. The kitchen suddenly seemed so small, as though there wasn't room for the both of them anymore.

"You can look at it any way you want," she said, taking a step backward. "But if they aren't all in on it, then they sure aren't stepping up to help. And every time you smile at one of them or shake one of their hands you are just making it that much easier for them to stab you in the back."

"Sabrina," Granny said. "You have to get a hold of your anger. If you cannot learn to control your hatred, your hatred will control you."

"I'll get a hold of my anger when my mom and dad are safe at home," the girl cried.

Sabrina spun around and rushed out of the room, up the stairs, and into her bedroom. She slammed the door and ran to her bed. Burying her head under the pillows, she broke into violent sobs. In two weeks it would be Christmas, the second Christmas since one of them—one of the Everafters—had kidnapped her parents. Why didn't anyone care about bringing them home? Why was she the only one who saw what was really going on in Ferryport Landing?

• • •

Sabrina awoke to a knocking on her bedroom door. She looked

over at the clock on the nightstand and realized it was already seven o'clock at night. She had been asleep for more than three hours. Still in her robe and socks, she crawled out of the bed and crossed the room to open the door. Mr. Canis was waiting on the other side.

"The family awaits you in the car," he said.

"I don't feel like going anywhere," she responded. The thought of seeing Granny Relda and Daphne right now made her sick to her stomach.

"Child, this is not an invitation," Mr. Canis said. "There is work to be done. Get dressed now and meet us at the car."

"Where are we going?"

Mr. Canis took a deep breath before he answered. "The answer to that question will not change the fact that you are going there. We are waiting in the car."

"I'll be down in a minute," Sabrina said. She closed the door and got dressed, but the fresh clothes didn't do anything to hide the horrible odor coming off of her. She had slept through bathtime, and now she smelled like a slimy, bottom-feeding fish.

She hurried through the empty house, put on her coat and hat, and opened the front door. Granny was waiting outside with her key ring in hand.

"Feeling better?" she asked.

Sabrina nodded. Thankfully, the old woman wasn't going to keep harping on their conversation.

"Good, a nap can do wonders for a person. Hurry along. Everyone is in the car."

Daphne, Elvis, and Puck were in the backseat looking warm and well fed. The little girl and the dog both stared out the window when Sabrina got inside. Apparently, her little sister was back to giving Sabrina the silent treatment, and this time Elvis was joining her. Puck, on the other hand, looked at her and laughed.

"You are in so much trouble." He chuckled, sounding impressed.

"Where are we going?" she asked.

"The sheriff needs our help," Granny replied.

They cruised through the country roads, heading toward the elementary school. Mr. Canis pulled into the parking lot. Sheriff Hamstead's car was parked nearby. When everyone piled out, the old man once again climbed onto the top of the car and sat in his meditative posture. Elvis whined when he realized he was being left behind again.

"Buddy, you can come in with us, but there's a criminal stealing blankets out of the backseats of cars," Daphne warned. "He might snatch yours while we're inside."

The big dog bit down hard on the edge of his blanket and eyed the windows suspiciously as the family went into the school.

They rushed to the principal's office, where they found the sheriff sitting in a chair taking notes while Mr. Hamelin paced back and forth.

"Relda, what are you doing here?" the principal asked.

"The sheriff asked us to come by," she explained.

"The Grimms are pretty good at finding people," Hamstead said awkwardly. It was obvious to Sabrina he was trying to be discreet about the family being deputized.

"We're happy to help," Granny Relda said.

"No offense, Relda, but my kid is freezing out in the cold somewhere. I don't need an old woman and two kids, I need the police department," Hamelin said.

"I've got the best tracking dog in the world in the car," Granny said. "I'd take Elvis over a hundred police officers any day. We'll find your boy."

The principal sat down in his chair and rolled it over to the icy window. "It's so cold out there," he whispered.

"My girls were chasing Wendell this afternoon," Granny said.

"I heard all about it," the man responded, without turning away from the window.

"Then you know he's involved with the deaths."

Hamelin spun around in his seat angrily and pointed his finger at the old woman. "He didn't do it," he shouted.

"I know that, Piper. In fact, I think he's been trying to stop what's going on in this school."

"He's so curious. One afternoon we watched an old black-and-white detective movie on TV together and he was hooked. Now, *everything's* a mystery. I should have known he'd get himself in trouble."

"He also seems to have picked up his father's flair for music. I hear he's using a harmonica to control animals."

"Relda, he's a good kid," Hamelin said.

Suddenly, there was a knock at the door and Mr. Sheepshank entered.

"Oh, hello, everyone. So sorry to interrupt," he said, pointing to the wristwatch on his freckled arm. "Mr. Hamelin, it's time."

"Counselor, my son is missing!" the principal shouted angrily. Sabrina turned to look at the rosy-cheeked man, who smiled nervously.

"Of course. We can talk later," he said. He closed the door and was gone.

Daphne took her silver star out of her pocket and pinned it to her chest so that everyone could see her badge. "Mr. Hamelin, we don't want you to worry. We'll find your son and bring him back to you."

Granny Relda smiled at the little girl.

"Why are you so eager to help me?" Hamelin asked.

"That's our job," Daphne said. "To protect and serve." The little girl reached down, yanked on her belt, and pulled her pants up. Sabrina almost burst out laughing, but quickly stopped herself when Sheriff Hamstead's angry face told her he recognized the little girl's impression.

"I know you've had a history with my family, Piper, but I like to think we're never too far along to start over," Granny said, extending her hand. Hamelin stared at it for a moment, then shook it firmly.

"All we need is his locker number."

The principal punched a key on his desktop computer and the screen lit up. He typed in a few strokes and smiled.

"He's number three-two-three. That's right around the corner, near the boiler room door," he said. "What should I do? Can I go with you?"

"Wait here," the sheriff said as he stood up from his chair. "We'll call you as soon as we know anything."

Hamstead and the family walked out of the office and down the hall until they found 323, right where the principal had told them it would be.

"Do you have some kind of magic that opens locks?" Sabrina asked, as she eyed the combination lock on the door.

Granny opened her handbag and pulled out a hammer.

"I wouldn't call it magic, exactly," she said, handing the hammer to Puck. The boy grinned and raised the hammer high over his head. He brought it down hard on the lock and it snapped in two.

"Can I do another?" he asked, but the old woman snatched the hammer out of his hand and placed it back into her handbag. Then she tossed the broken pieces of the lock to the floor and opened the locker. Inside was a winter coat Wendell had left behind. Granny pulled it out and tucked it under her arm.

"I really appreciate this," the sheriff said.

"Don't think twice about it," the old woman said.

Back in the parking lot, the Grimms and Puck found Mr. Canis still meditating on the roof of the jalopy.

"We're heading into the forest," Granny said, opening the back door and letting Elvis out. "Why don't you stay here in case Wendell wanders back to the school."

"Are you sure you won't be needing me?" the old man said.

"We've got this one handled," Granny Relda said.

"Can I ask you a question, Mr. Canis?" Daphne asked.

"Of course, little one."

"What do you think about when you're sitting on top of the car?"

Mr. Canis thought for a moment, then looked up at the moon, now high over the nearby forest. "I concentrate on all the people I hurt when I was unable to control myself."

"And that helps you stay calm?" Sabrina asked.

"No child, it helps remind me of my guilt," he replied.

Sabrina didn't know a lot of fairy-tale stories. Her dad used to say fairy tales were pointless. When other kids were reading about the Little Mermaid and Beauty and the Beast, her father was discussing the news with his daughters or reading them the Sunday comics using different voices for the characters. Sabrina and Daphne had done their fairy-tale reading on the sly or at school. Still, everyone knew the story of Little Red Riding Hood, and as Sabrina looked at Mr. Canis, a terrible realization ran through her. This man sitting on the car roof, who slept across the hall from them at night, had killed an old woman once upon a time. Only it wasn't a story, it had really happened. He'd tried to eat a child, too. How could Granny let him live in the house? No wonder her dad had forbidden even a copy of *Mother Goose* from entering their home. He was trying to protect them from the truth.

Granny was busy holding Wendell's coat under Elvis's nose. The giant dog took a deep lung full and was soon trotting across the school lawn, sniffing madly in the grass.

"Looks like he's got the scent, *lieblings*," Granny said. "Let's go find our Wendell."

0

lvis's big feet crunched on the hard ground. The night had grown bitterly cold and every once in a while Sabrina spotted a snowflake floating toward the ground. She was freezing, even in her heavy coat. If Wendell was still alive out in the woods without his, it would be a miracle.

Elvis sniffed the air. Once the big dog caught a scent, he never lost it. When he reached the edge of the trees, he stopped and barked impatiently at the family. It was obvious they were slowing him down.

"Oh, I wish I could bottle his energy," Granny Relda said, taking Sabrina's arm in order to help herself across the school's icy lawn. "I'd be a rich old lady."

When they finally reached Elvis, he led them into the woods. He sniffed wildly, rushing back and forth along a path, following the scent, but managing to stick close to the family, as if he knew the old woman would have a difficult time keeping up with his pace.

Sabrina heard a branch snap in the distance and saw the dog's keen ears perk up. She expected him to run off howling in the direction of the sound, but instead he continued to follow his invisible path.

It seemed as if they had been searching for hours and Sabrina's toes were getting numb. Puck complained and suggested that they give up several times, insisting that Wendell's rabbit army had probably turned on him and were now feasting on his chubby body. Sabrina was also ready to give up, when they came to a small clearing and a sight so incredible even Granny Relda gasped.

On the ground at their feet was a mound of fur nearly four feet high and six feet wide. At first, Sabrina thought it might be a small bear, but as they got closer they realized it wasn't a single animal, but a group of many. In fact, it was a pile of rabbits huddling together in the cold. Elvis growled at the pile, but if the little forest animals noticed, they chose to ignore him.

"I told you!" Puck cried. "His woodland army mutinied! I hope he was delicious, little rodents!"

The old woman stepped close to the pile and leaned down. "Wendell!"

The mound stirred for a moment but then became totally still.

"Wendell! Your father is worried sick about you," Granny Relda scolded. "Now come out of there this instant."

"No!" a voice shouted from the depths of the rabbits. "You're going to take me to jail. I won't go."

"No one is taking you to jail, Wendell," Granny said. "All we want to do is take you home."

The mound stirred and shivered. A brief note from the boy's harmonica was heard and suddenly the rabbits rushed off in different directions.

"Run, you dirty little carrot-munchers," Puck shouted after them. "But know today that your kind has made an enemy of the Trickster King!"

When they were all gone, Wendell lay at the family's feet. Granny stepped forward, helped the boy up, and got him into his coat.

"I didn't do it," he insisted.

"Then why did you run?" Sabrina asked.

"And send rabbits to eat us! I'm a seven-year-old girl," Daphne said. "Do you know how important bunny rabbits are to me?"

"I didn't think you'd believe me. I knew how it looked, but I was trying to stop them," the boy pleaded. "If I had gotten in trouble, it would have ruined all my work so far."

He shoved his hand into his coat pocket and pulled out a business card. He handed it to Granny. The old woman read it, looked impressed, and nodded at him.

Sabrina took the card and read it closely. It said, WENDELL EMORY HAMELIN, PRIVATE INVESTIGATOR. At the bottom of the card was a magnifying glass with a huge eye inside it.

"So, you're a detective," Granny Relda said with a smile.

Daphne snatched the card and studied it. "I want a business card, too."

"Something terrible is happening inside the school," Wendell said. "I'm trying to find whoever's responsible and stop them."

"We know. Why don't you tell us everything on the way back to the school," the old woman said. "Your father is there waiting for you."

The group trudged back through the forest and Wendell told them all he had learned.

"I was leaving the school yesterday, when I looked back and saw something happening in Mr. Grumpner's room," he said, stopping to blow his nose into his handkerchief. "Sorry, I've got really bad allergies."

"It's OK, go on," Granny Relda replied.

"Like I was saying, Grumpner fell backward over some desks and at first I thought he might be sick, but then a monster attacked him. I was kind of far away, so I couldn't really see, but it looked like a giant spider. It grabbed Grumpner and started covering him in its sticky web. Well, I remembered from science class that birds are a spider's natural predator."

"What's a *predator*?" Daphne asked.

"It's like a hunter," Sabrina replied.

"So, I got out a harmonica I'd bought and blew into it as hard as I could," the boy continued. "I didn't even know if it would work. Dad told me to never do it. He said musical instruments were off limits on account of his past. Please don't tell him I bought the harmonica. He'll get real mad."

Granny took his hand. "Don't worry, Wendell."

He relaxed and continued. "So, I just thought of birds and before I knew it the sky was full of them. They were looking at me like I was their leader or something, and it took me a while to realize they were looking for instructions, so I pointed at the window and said 'Save Mr. Grumpner'."

"How come you remember Mr. Grumpner?" Sabrina asked. "The rest of our class doesn't."

"My dad had a protection spell put on our house. Whenever they dust the town, we aren't affected.

"So, anyway, the birds went straight for the window and smashed it. They flew in and attacked the monster. Unfortunately, it was too late. Even from out in the yard, I could see the spider had already eaten him."

"That explains the feathers," Daphne said.

"And what about the janitor?" Sabrina asked, still not sure she believed the strange boy's story.

"Ms. Spangler gave me a detention for refusing to play dodgeball," Wendell said. "I mean, we know how to play the game. Let's move on, already. So, when I walked in, there was this ugly, hairy thing fighting with Mrs. Heart and Ms. White. At first I thought it was a bear, but it moved way too fast and it had these weird yellow eyes. Mrs. Heart was pretty useless against it. She hid behind a desk and screamed while Ms. White fought the thing. I got my harmonica out, wondering if I could control it, too, and at first it seemed to work, but it ran to the window, opened it, and leaped outside. When you guys saw me, I wasn't running away, I was trying to catch it."

"You're quite brave, Wendell," Granny Relda said.

"My line of work isn't for the faint of heart," he declared, wiping his nose on his handkerchief.

"We've also had a run-in with an unusual creature," the old woman said.

"I know this is going to sound crazy, but I don't think these creatures are monsters. I think they're the children of Everafters."

"That's an excellent deduction," said Granny Relda. "You've got the makings of a great detective."

The boy smiled. "The only thing I wasn't sure about was why the attacks were taking place in the first place. That is, until I found the tunnels."

"Tunnels!" Sabrina and Daphne cried.

"Yes, someone is digging under the school. They start in the boiler room and go on for a long time. I'm sure it's all connected—the tunnels, the giant spider, hairy things. I just don't know how."

"Perhaps we should team up," Granny Relda said. "Combining our efforts might solve the case sooner."

"Sorry, lady, I work alone," Wendell said as they reached the front door of the school. "Detective work is dangerous business. I don't want any dames getting in the way."

Sabrina rolled her eyes. *Someone's been watching too many detective movies, all right,* she thought.

"I understand," Granny said, trying her best to sound disappointed, just as Mr. Hamelin came running down the hallway. He swooped his boy up in his arms and hugged him.

"Do you know how worried your mother and I have been?" his father said, half lecturing and half laughing.

"I'm sorry, Dad," the boy said. "But there's a caper afoot, and I'm in the thick of it."

"Thank you, Relda," Mr. Hamelin said, reaching over and kissing the old woman on the cheek. "Thank you all."

Daphne tugged on her pants and stepped forward, mimicking the sheriff's funny little bow-legged walk. "Just doing my job, citizen," she said.

"You're welcome," Sabrina added.

"I've heard stories that you have a harmonica, young man," the principal said, reaching his hand out to the boy.

Wendell frowned. "But I need it," he argued. "It helps with my detective work."

"You're about to retire," his father said, sternly. "Until these monsters are caught, your days as a detective are over."

Wendell reached into his pocket and pulled out his shiny harmonica. He reluctantly handed it to his father and grimaced when Hamelin stuffed it into his pants pocket.

"Mr. Hamelin, before we go, I was wondering something," Sabrina said. "Are there any more children here at the school like Wendell?"

"What do you mean?" the principal asked.

"You know, children of Everafters?"

"He's the only one I know of."

"Anyone else on the staff?"

"Only Ms. White, myself, and now Mrs. Heart," Hamelin said. "About ten years ago Ms. Muffet, the Beast, and the Frog Prince were all on staff, but they went in on a lottery ticket and won millions of dollars and quit. I was happy for them but it was a real shame. Good teachers are hard to find."

"Anyone else?"

"I, uh, I'm not sure," Hamelin said. "They don't really come with tags. I suppose there might be a couple, but I wouldn't know."

"Of course," Granny Relda said. She looked at Sabrina and the girl saw a sparkle in her eye, the kind her grandmother got when she found an important clue. "Is there a phone I could use?"

The principal gestured toward his door. "There's one in the secretary's office."

"Thank you," Granny said, slipping out the door. "Children, I'll be right back."

The group stared at one another in awkward silence.

At last Puck spoke. "So, Piper, how many rats were there?" he asked, referring to the man's famous adventure.

"Thousands," the principal replied.

"That's gross," Daphne groaned.

Granny returned to the room and smiled. "Well, we have to be going, now," she said, turning to Wendell. "Try to stay out of trouble."

"Trouble would be wise to stay out of my way," the boy said, sounding like a movie detective.

As the family walked back down the hall, they passed the boiler room.

"We should check the tunnels now while no one is here," Sabrina suggested, walking over to the boiler room door and trying the knob. It was locked.

"No, if people are being killed to protect what's in them, I suggest we take the hint for now," Granny Relda replied. "At least until we find out who these murderers are. In the meantime, I think I know the parents of our killers. Let's have a chat with them."

• • •

A skinny Christmas tree sat at the entrance to the police station. It was hung with a few strands of tinsel and had a garland wrapped sloppily around it. A couple of boxes of shiny bulbs sat underneath it, waiting to be strung on the tree's limbs. As they passed the display, Sabrina finally realized how overworked the sheriff was. He didn't even have time to finish his holiday decorations.

Sheriff Hamstead was at the front desk, surrounded by six of the most unusual people Sabrina had ever seen. She recognized two of them immediately. Beauty and the Beast weren't a couple she would soon forget. The dazzlingly gorgeous Beauty was a complete contrast to her husband, the fur-covered, fang-faced Beast. As for the others in the room, there was a pretty blond woman in a tiara and satiny blue gown standing next to a tall, strong man with enormous green eyes and an odd scaly skin disorder. The Frog Prince, Sabrina realized. Next to them was a chubby woman covered in jewels, Little Miss Muffet, holding hands, or in this case, holding the leg, of an enormous black spider nearly the size of Elvis. All six of them were complaining and shouting at the sheriff.

"What's the meaning of this, Hamstead?" the Beast growled.

"We had dinner reservations at Old King Cole's," Beauty cried. "Do you know how long it takes to get a table at Christmastime? We called in September!"

The Frog Prince's bride was as angry as anyone. "Drag me out of my home in the middle of the night," she huffed. "We're royalty!"

"It's beyond rude," the scaly Frog Prince complained.

The spider clicked angrily with its gigantic pincers.

"Settle down, everyone," the sheriff shouted, as he stood up. "Relda Grimm will explain everything."

"What? Since when does Relda Grimm run the police force?" Little Miss Muffet demanded. Her spider companion clicked and hissed in protest.

"The mayor has asked my family to help with the investigation of the two murders at Ferryport Landing Elementary," Granny replied.

Little Miss Muffet stepped forward. "What's that got to do with us?" she asked.

"Miss Muffet, it has everything to do with you," the old woman replied. "And your children."

The crowd gasped and averted their eyes.

"Relda Grimm, you've lost your mind," the Beast declared. "None of us have children."

"That's what I thought," Granny Relda said. "Until my granddaughter asked a question that I should have asked myself. 'Who else worked at Ferryport Landing Elementary?' I had nearly forgotten that you, the Frog Prince, and Little Miss Muffet were all teachers there before the three of you won the lottery."

Sabrina beamed with pride. Granny may have disapproved of Sabrina's suspicions about the Everafters, but it was those same suspicions that were helping solve the mystery.

"We won the lottery more than ten years ago," Miss Muffet said. "And I go by Mrs. Arachnid now."

"So we worked at the school. What does that have to do with the murder?" the Frog Prince asked.

"It's your retirement that interests me. Let me explain. Witnesses say there have been attacks by two so-called monsters on school grounds," Granny said, crossing the room and stopping in front of the Frog Prince and Princess. "And my family and I were victims of a third attack during our investigation. This one involved a half-girl, half-frog creature. Luckily, no one was hurt."

The couple lowered their eyes and Granny moved on to Muffet, aka Mrs. Arachnid, and her spider. "Unfortunately, I can't say the same for Mr. Grumpner. He was killed by what we suspect was a giant spider."

The spider clicked angrily, but his wife was still. Granny moved on to Beauty and the Beast.

"Charlie, the school janitor, also met an untimely demise by a creature described as a hairy, man-eating beast with yellow eyes," Granny said.

"You can't prove those are our children," Beauty cried.

"You're right, but there is one thing that we can prove," Sheriff Hamstead interjected. "None of you ever won the lottery."

Everyone gasped, even Puck.

"I called the state lottery commission," the sheriff continued. "They have records of every lottery winner in the last one hundred years. None of you are on their lists."

"Where did you get the money?" Granny asked.

"Are you suggesting we sold our children?" the Beast growled.

"I think you know I am," Granny Relda answered.

"And so am I," Hamstead added. He reached into his pocket and took out a pair of handcuffs. "I also think you are going to be arrested unless someone starts talking."

"We were nearly broke when we found out I was pregnant," the Frog Princess said. "All of our money was gone; we were worried we'd lose our house. If you go broke in Ferryport Landing, you stay that way. There's no one to bail you out. You can't move to another town. We would have been beggars in the street."

Beauty broke down in tears, as well. "We were in the same predicament, barely making ends meet on Beast's teacher's salary. It was no way to raise a child. He told us he could help.

"One night, he brought over a spinning wheel and started spinning gold. By morning, we had enough to last us a dozen lifetimes. We sold it to a precious metals merchant from New York City. We were rich overnight."

"Who did this?" said Granny Relda.

"Rumpelstiltskin," the Frog Princess cried. The Frog Prince took her hand and begged her to be silent, but the tears and truth were already pouring out of her. "We had to come up with an explanation for the money, so we invented the lottery story," she said.

"You sold your children?" Sabrina cried. She had never heard a more horrible story in her entire life. "How could you!"

"He manipulated us," Mrs. Arachnid sobbed. "I know you don't understand, but when we gave him the babies it was like we weren't in control of ourselves. We were so desperate, so full of despair. It was like he crawled into our brains and rewired them so we really believed it was the best thing we could do."

"No, I don't understand," Sabrina shouted. "You filthy Everafters are nothing but animals! You would hand your children over to a monster so you could cover yourselves in jewels and furs!"

Mrs. Arachnid looked down at her sparkling necklace and started to cry.

"Sabrina," Granny said. "That's enough."

"I agree," Daphne said. "Take a chill pill."

Sabrina ignored them. "No wonder Wilhelm trapped you in this town. All of you belong in a cage!"

"*Sabrina Grimm, you will hold your tongue this instant!*" Granny Relda ordered.

"You got yelled at," Puck taunted.

"*Puck, that goes for you as well!*"

Sabrina was stunned. The old woman had never raised her voice to her. The girl's face was hot with embarrassment.

"If we showed you photos of all the children at the school, do you think you could pick out which ones might be yours in their human disguise?" the sheriff asked, picking up the Ferryport Landing Elementary School yearbook that was sitting on his desk.

"I don't think so, Ernest," Beauty said, trying to control her sobbing. "We haven't seen them since they were a day old. We didn't even get to name them."

"Well, we will do the best we can to reunite you with them," Granny Relda said.

"You would do that for us?" the Beast asked.

"Of course," Daphne said proudly. "We are Grimms and this is what we do."

"Do you need anything from me?" Hamstead said.

Granny shook her head and flashed Sabrina an angry look.

"Actually, can I have a police hat?" Daphne asked the sheriff. Hamstead smiled and nodded at the girl.

"You are so punk rock!" she cried.

• • •

Once the family was outside, Sabrina wasn't sure which was colder—the bitter winter air or Granny's attitude toward her. She also knew that Daphne was going to give her the silent treatment again. But it didn't matter to her anymore.

"I'm not sorry for what I said," she declared.

"Oh, we're well aware of that," Granny Relda said as they approached the car. Mr. Canis was waiting on the roof.

"I heard yelling," he said, crawling down to help the old woman into the front seat.

"I bet you're going to hear a lot more," Puck said, sounding hopeful.

"Everything is fine," the old woman said. "It is late and I think we all need a good night of rest."

"Good idea," Daphne said. "We can search the tunnels tomorrow."

"No, I don't think so," Granny said as they got settled into the car. "Things have escalated to a point where I don't feel comfortable having the three of you help out. A few Everafter children are one thing, but Rumpelstiltskin is another entirely.

He may be behind these murders, and he's one of the most deranged and mysterious fairy-tale creatures that ever came to Ferryport Landing. I can't put you into harm's way when I have no idea what to expect."

"This isn't about danger," Sabrina said, shaking with anger and hurt. "We've been in plenty of dangerous situations since we moved to this town. This is about me, isn't it?"

Granny Relda turned in her seat and eyed the girl. "In the past, I thought you two girls were smart enough to handle yourselves. I thought you might possibly be the cleverest Grimms in the history of the family, but right now, I don't trust your judgment, Sabrina. You're not who I thought you were, child. I'm sorry, but this case is closed for the sisters Grimm."

• • •

Everyone was furious with her, so Sabrina had crept upstairs to her room, rather than hear another lecture. As she lay in bed, looking up at the model airplanes her father had hung from the ceiling, she thought there might be an upside to being the black sheep of the family. While everyone was busy solving mysteries, she could spend more time searching for her parents. Just two days ago, she would have thought this was a perfect chance, but now, with Granny acting so blind to the truth about the town's residents, she worried the old woman would be their next victim. If that happened, the girls would get sent back to the orphanage and any chance of finding their mom and dad would be gone.

Daphne entered the room, dressed in her pajamas, and sat down on the edge of the bed.

"Well, we now know what Granny's like when she's mad," she said. "She's downstairs cleaning the house. She's been dusting for the last hour. If you get her any madder, she's going to clean out the closets."

"I didn't mean to make her angry," Sabrina said.

"You've got to get over this thing you have about Everafters," Daphne said.

Sabrina groaned. If Daphne was going to lecture her, she'd be happy to go back to receiving the silent treatment.

"No, what I've got to do is convince everyone to stop being so naïve," Sabrina said. "But let's just say I'm wrong about everything. Punishing us for my attitude isn't going to help solve the case. Granny can't do it all, and she's not going to get any help from Charming and the sheriff. We could be searching the tunnels. Who knows how far they've dug, or even what they're digging for? Maybe there's some kind of monster under the town. I know that sounds nuts, but we used to think the same thing about giants not so long ago. What if the bad guys are doing something really bad down there while Granny is running around trying to find out which of the kids at school are monsters?"

"So what do we do?"

"We do what we're supposed to do," Sabrina said. "We're Grimms and something is wrong in this town. It's our job to find out what it is."

• • •

Once she was confident her grandmother and Mr. Canis were asleep, Sabrina shook her sister awake and the two of them crawled out of bed. They crept out of their room and down the hall to Puck's bedroom.

"Don't step on the plate," Sabrina reminded her sister as she opened the door. Inside the boy's magical forest room, the sun had set, replaced by a sea of stars, each blinking brightly just for Puck. The boxing kangaroo was asleep in his ring and the roller coaster had been turned off. All was still, except for the cascading waterfall splashing into the lagoon.

The girls crept along the path around the lagoon and then into some heavy brush. Eventually, they came to a trampoline on which Puck was sound asleep. The Trickster King was wearing a pair of baby blue footie pajamas that had little smiling stars and moons on them. Held close to his face was a soft pink stuffed unicorn with a rainbow sewn on its side. If only Sabrina had brought a camera, she could have also recorded his thumb in his mouth.

"Time to wake up the sleepy monkey," Sabrina cooed in baby talk, doing her best not to roar with laughter.

Daphne giggled but held her hand over her mouth.

"Wakie-wakie, eggs and bac-ie," Sabrina continued.

Puck stirred in his sleep but didn't wake. A big stream of drool escaped his mouth and ran down the front of his pajamas.

"Does someone have the sleepy-sleepies?" Daphne said mimicking her sister's baby talk.

"Time to come back from dreamland, precious," the older girl said, shaking the boy roughly. Puck sprang from his sleep, with wings extended from his back. He waved his big pink unicorn like a deadly sword and slashed at the children.

"Nice jammies," Daphne snickered.

"I especially like Mr. Unicorn," Sabrina laughed.

"His name is Kraven the Deceiver," Puck corrected, before realizing what he was holding and who was with him. He tossed the stuffed animal aside and fluttered down to the ground.

"We've got a plan for tomorrow and you're going to help us," Sabrina said.

"Forget it," the boy answered. "Tomorrow I'm telling the old lady to find another bodyguard for her stinky offspring. It's beneath me!"

"But this plan requires a lot of a mischief," Sabrina said.

Puck's eyes lit up. "I'm listening," he said.

"We're going to get into the boiler room tomorrow to search the tunnels."

"The old lady will be furious."

"I know, but I'm willing to take the heat if it saves someone's life."

"Fine, what's the plan?"

Sabrina reached into her pocket and took out her set of keys.

"Where'd you get those?" Daphne asked.

"I've been swiping them off Granny's key ring one by one and making copies at the hardware store."

Puck's eyes lit up and he looked at Sabrina as if he had never seen her before in his life. "You stole those keys and made copies?"

She dropped her eyes. "Yeah," she said, thinking she felt disapproval.

"That's wonderful," the boy said, eyeing the girl like a child watching a fireworks display. He was in complete awe of her. He grabbed both the girls by the wrist and dragged them through his "room." "Let's put them to use, then!"

Once they were in Mirror's room, the three children stepped

through the reflection and came out into the Hall of Wonders. Mirror was standing in front of his own full-length mirror, sucking in his plump belly and making muscle poses like a body builder.

"Doesn't anyone in this house sleep anymore?" he asked.

"We need some help," Sabrina said.

The little man rolled his eyes and let out his belly. "Very well, what's the scoop?"

"We need something that will help us get into the boiler room at school," Daphne said. "The door is locked, so we need something that will turn us invisible or let us walk through walls."

"Children, this isn't Wal-Mart," Mirror replied. "I don't have everything, but there is something that might help. Follow me."

As they followed Mirror down the long hallway, Sabrina read the golden plaques on each of the doors, a favorite habit developed on previous visits: LEPRECHAUN GOLD; FLOOR PLANS FOR GINGERBREAD HOUSES; TALKING FISH; GHOSTS OF CHRISTMAS PAST, PRESENT, AND FUTURE; TIK-TOK MEN; CALIBAN—the doors went on and on. What was Mirror going to offer them?

Soon, he stopped at a door with a plaque that read THE PANTRY. He held out his hand and Sabrina gave him her key ring. He searched through her collection and found the one that unlocked the door. Everyone stepped inside where, much to the girls' chagrin, there stood an old, run-down refrigerator.

"I've never heard of the magic refrigerator," Daphne said. "Is that a Grimm story or someone else?"

"There's no such thing as a magic refrigerator," Mirror said as he opened the door. "It's what's inside that's important."

He opened the fridge, bent down, and rummaged around inside. He pulled out a bag of rotten carrots. "I really have to toss these out," he mumbled. He opened a carton of milk and took a sniff, his face crinkling up in disgust as he closed the carton and put it back in the refrigerator. Finally, he took out a package of juice boxes and handed them to the kids.

"Drink me," Daphne read.

"This is from *Alice's Adventures in Wonderland*," Sabrina said, happily. "This will make us shrink?"

"To about the size of an ant," Mirror said. "At that size you could just walk under the door and get into any room you want. But you'll need these, too." He reached in and pulled out several individually wrapped snack cakes. They looked just like the kind Sabrina used to buy at the deli near their Manhattan apartment, but the label said, EAT ME!

"These will make you big, but don't eat too many, they're not exactly Atkins friendly," Mirror warned. "Tweedle-Dee and Tweedle-Dum sold these for a week at their convenience store before your grandmother confiscated their stock. The town was filled with giant children. It took us a week to sort it out."

"We'll need four of each, I think," Sabrina said.

"But there's only three of us," Daphne argued.

"I have a feeling the great detective Wendell Hamelin is going to change his mind about being a loner," her sister replied.

• • •

The next day at school, the trio walked down the crowded hallway toward the boiler room. Sabrina scrutinized every kid along the way. Any one of them could be a giant spider or a frog-girl, but besides being exhausted, they all looked just like every other kid Sabrina had ever seen. At least her suspicions about Wendell proved correct. He was waiting for them by the doorway with a handkerchief and a runny nose.

"I've been doing some thinking and I believe that joining forces might be a great idea, but under a couple of conditions," he said, rushing to join the group.

"What conditions?" Sabrina said.

"I handle all the dangerous work," the chubby boy said, puffing up his chest like a tough guy.

The children looked at one another and fought off a laugh.

"Fine," Sabrina said. "I think we should have a look in the tunnels right away."

"I agree, but there's a problem," Wendell said, wiping his nose again. "They changed the locks on the boiler room door."

Sabrina reached into her backpack and tossed the boy an Eat Me cake and a Drink Me juice box.

"What are these?" he asked.

"The key to the new lock."

"You want to do it now?" Daphne cried. "Ms. White will notice I'm gone and come looking for me."

"We'll worry about that later," said her sister. "Lunchtime is too busy and the bad guys will probably be watching after school. We'll wait until the bell rings for class and once the hall is empty, we'll get started."

Soon enough, the bell rang, and the kids filed into their classes. Sabrina, Daphne, Puck, and Wendell milled around, trying to appear as if they were on their way to class without actually going anywhere.

Once they were alone in the hall, the children took out their Drink Me boxes and inserted the handy straws attached to the sides.

"How much do we drink?" Daphne asked, sniffing at the box.

"I don't know," Sabrina said. "I guess until it starts working."

Puck took a long slurp and when he was finished he opened his mouth and belched. "It's fruity," he exclaimed. Suddenly, to a sound like that of a squeaky balloon losing its air, his body shrank to half its size. Even his clothes, the Eat Me cake, and the juice box got tiny.

"Drink more," Daphne insisted. "You aren't small enough to get under the door."

"And hurry up," Sabrina said, scanning the hallway. The last thing she wanted was a teacher or student to see this craziness.

Puck took another sip and shrank even further. Soon, he was no taller than a quarter standing on its end. Sabrina bent down and examined the tiny boy.

"You have no idea how tempted I am to squish you," she said.

"And you have no idea how big your nose hairs are," he squeaked. Sabrina covered her face with her hand.

"Our turn," Daphne said. The three other children took big sips out of their boxes and in no time they were all shrinking, too. The liquid did taste fruity, like pineapples and cherry pie at the same time. A cool tingle ran down Sabrina's throat, into her belly, and then into her legs and arms. The sensation wasn't unlike having a good stretch after a wonderful night's sleep. When she finished the box, she was the same size as Puck.

"Let's get in there before we wind up on the bottom of someone's shoe," said the tiny Wendell. He marched over to the door and looked back. "I'll go first, in case there's something waiting for us on the other side."

He yanked out his hanky, blew hard on it, then shoved it back into his pocket. Then he walked underneath the door without even having to bend over. Daphne took Sabrina's hand and together they followed Wendell, with Puck bringing up the rear.

"I should be doing the dangerous stuff," he grumbled.

Once the group was on the other side, the children had a chance to look around. A bucket full of mops sat in the corner, boxes of trash bags and rolls of toilet paper filled a nearby shelf, and an ancient coal furnace rested in the center of the room. Not far off, a brand-new electric furnace clicked and popped as it pushed warm air throughout the vents of the school. But what was bewildering was how gigantic everything was. The mops looked as tall as the Empire State Building in midtown New York City and Sabrina suspected if one of the rolls of toilet paper were to fall off the shelf and on to them, they'd be crushed to death.

"Look at that table," Daphne cried, pointing at a nearby desk. "It's huge."

Sabrina nodded in agreement.

"Look at that chair," Daphne said. "It's huge!"

Sabrina agreed.

"Look at that button!" Daphne said, running over to a monstrous white button that had fallen off of someone's shirt. She tried to lift it, but it was too heavy for her in her shrunken state. "It's huge!"

"We need to find you another word," Sabrina muttered.

"Hey! I'm seven! I don't know a lot of words," the little girl said.

"All right, piggy," Puck said to Wendell. "Where's the entrance to the tunnel?"

"We need to eat the cakes and get big," the boy detective said. "The lever that opens the entrance is in the old furnace."

The children reached in their pockets for their Eat Me cakes when suddenly, the boiler room door opened.

"Someone's coming!" Sabrina shouted. The door closed and a man walked over to the coal furnace. He opened a small trapdoor on its side and reached in. Sabrina guessed he had pushed the lever because a hum filled the room, and the coal furnace began to slide across the floor. That's when Sabrina noticed it was Principal Hamelin.

The principal waited patiently, and when the coal furnace had slid away, he descended a flight of stairs hidden underneath the machine.

The children rushed to the center of the room.

"That was your dad," Sabrina said to Wendell.

"What is he doing?" he said.

"We have to follow him," Daphne insisted.

"We can't! If we eat the cakes and get big, he's sure to spot us, but at this size we'll never make it down those steps," her sister argued.

"No worries, girls. I have a brilliant plan," Puck said, proudly. He spun around on his heels and transformed into an elephant, albeit a tiny elephant. He let out a mighty roar and charged off into the far corner of the room.

"Puck, we don't have time for your stupidity," Sabrina shouted after him, but the boy-elephant did not respond. Soon, she could hear the scraping of metal on the floor. When elephant Puck returned he was pushing a dustpan with his massive head, all the way to the edge of the steps. When the pan was on the edge of the top step, the elephant morphed back into the boy.

"Get in," he said, beaming with pride.

Sabrina looked at the dustpan hanging precariously over the edge. "No way," she said. "We'll kill ourselves in that thing."

Daphne was already climbing inside and had found a spot in the corner to sit down. "We survived Granny's driving," she said. "We'll survive this, too."

"You'll be fine," Puck assured Sabrina. "You'll probably need someone to feed you for the rest of your life, but you'll make it. Stop being a baby and get in."

Sabrina looked at Wendell. He shrugged and the two of them climbed into the dustpan.

"You all need to stay in the back of this thing," Puck explained. "Oh, and one more thing . . ."

"What?" Sabrina cried. She didn't like the tone of his voice.

"Buckle up, kiddies," Puck shouted as he walked to the front of the pan and leaped into the air. His body came down hard on the end of the pan and the back tilted high in the air, sending the whole thing rocketing down the steps before Sabrina could even scream. Each step it cleared just made the dustpan increase its speed, until finally they crashed at the bottom of the stairs.

After Sabrina checked everyone for broken bones, she punched Puck in the arm.

"Hey, I got us here, didn't I?" he complained as he rubbed his sore shoulder.

The children climbed out of the dustpan, calmed themselves, and headed down a long, cavernous hall carved out of stone. Along the rocky path were pickaxes and dusty shovels, old buckets and miles and miles of rope.

What are they up to down here? Sabrina wondered, as everyone marched through the tunnel. The journey wouldn't have taken long if they were their usual size, but the length of a normal step now required a dozen.

"This is as far as I went before," Wendell said when they reached a place where the tunnels branched off into two directions. "Which way should we go?"

Sabrina heard voices arguing in the tunnel to the left.

"There's someone else down here besides your father," she said. "Let's go find out who."

The children followed the tunnel to the left, turned a corner, and crept as close as they could to the two men arguing in the dark. Sabrina couldn't make out the other person's face, but Hamelin was one of them for sure. The principal was wringing his hands.

"I'm telling you again. This has gone too far. No one was supposed to die," Hamelin said.

"Piper, you worry too much," a creaky voice said. To Sabrina, it sounded like the voice of a man who had been alive a thousand years without drinking a single sip of water. "Tonight we're going to reach our goal. We would already be there if it weren't for last night."

"My son was missing!" Hamelin cried. "What was I supposed to do?"

"Of all people, I understand," the voice crackled. "After all, I'm a father, too. The difference is that my children understand how important this is, while your child just gets in the way and puts this all at risk."

"Don't threaten me," the principal growled. "My boy isn't going to ruin our plans."

"Then we understand each other," the voice said. "Tonight we'll push forward, if you can find the time."

Hamelin's voice was so angry it was shaking. "Don't question my dedication. This was my idea after all."

"I'm glad to see you still remember that."

Hamelin spun around and rushed back up the tunnel, narrowly missing stepping on his own son, who just managed to leap out of the way.

"Are you OK?" Daphne asked, taking Wendell's hand in her own.

"I can't believe it," the boy said.

"We should go farther into the tunnel," Sabrina suggested. "We need to know where they are digging to." Everyone agreed, but just then something crawled out from around a corner and stopped the group in their tracks. An enormous brown mouse as big as a semi truck lumbered toward them. The rodent's pink nose and whiskers flicked and twitched as it sniffed at the children. Sabrina knew that at their current size they'd make a great snack for the hungry mouse.

"Eat the cakes," Sabrina advised, eyeing the mouse.

The children unwrapped their cakes and were just about to eat them when the mouse barreled forward and knocked Sabrina down. Daphne screamed and Puck leaped forward and dragged Sabrina to her feet. Unfortunately, she had dropped her cake right in front of the beast. The mouse spotted it, sniffed it, and with a quick flick of its tongue, ate it.

"That was a bad thing, wasn't it?" Sabrina said, sheepishly.

"Oh, man," Puck said, quickly shoving his own little chocolate cake into his mouth. "This is going to be awesome."

Daphne and Wendell were already munching their cakes, too, when Puck offered Sabrina his pinky.

"Hang on Sabrina," Puck said, flashing his devilish grin. "This is about to get interesting."

Sabrina grabbed his pinky finger and held it tightly just as the first changes affected the mouse's body. It sounded as if someone were blowing up a balloon. A ripple rolled across the mouse's skin and its eyes widened as its body inflated by a thousand times, yet its little legs and head stayed the exact same size, causing its massive body to plop to the ground. This was followed by a loud, squeaky rubber sound as the rodent's feet, legs, and head expanded in size. The children dashed down the tunnel to avoid the quickly expanding mouse.

Puck, meanwhile, was growing in the same awkward manner. His legs got big first, pushing him to his normal height and sending Sabrina soaring high into the air. When his upper body and hands finally followed, his pinky got thicker. Sabrina held on with all her might. Luckily, Puck was paying attention. He quickly swung her into his shirt pocket, where she clung to the top, just as Puck's head inflated.

Meanwhile, Daphne's head and feet were the first to inflate and the not-so-little girl hobbled around like a pumpkin that had suddenly sprouted shoes and was making an escape from the patch.

"I don't like this at all," she groaned. No sooner had she complained than her legs sprouted up like over-eager cornstalks, followed by her upper body, and lastly her neck. Wendell experienced the same kind of disturbing growth.

"It's all good," the runny-nosed detective announced, checking for all ten fingers. But what he didn't see was that it wasn't "all good." The mouse was also getting bigger and bigger until it was nearly as wide as the tunnel, and worse, it seemed very, very angry.

Puck grabbed Daphne and Daphne grabbed Wendell and they all rushed down the tunnel and up the stairs. When they got to the top, Daphne and Wendell raced across the room to the door, unlocked it, and hurried into the hall. Puck followed close behind, giggling like an idiot.

"Do you laugh every time we're in trouble?" Sabrina shouted.

The boy looked down into his pocket. "What are you squeaking about?"

When he was safely in the hall, Puck slammed the door shut and the children leaned against the walls on either side to catch their breath.

"I don't think we have to worry about him anymore," Puck said.

Just then, the door flew off its hinges, slammed against the opposite wall, and fell heavily to the floor. The giant mouse lumbered into the hallway and roared angrily. It was as big as a stuffed buffalo Sabrina had seen at the Natural History Museum. It let out a deafening squeak and licked its gigantic front teeth. To make matters worse, the dismissal bell rang and every classroom door opened. The hallway was immediately flooded with a sea of noisy children, eager to get to their next class. The mouse stomped hard, creating a chasm in the shiny floor, and all conversation ended abruptly.

"Well, piglet, you wanted to do the dangerous stuff," Puck laughed, as he turned to a stunned Wendell. "Be my guest!"

9

OK, everyone, there's no need to panic. We're professionals and we know how to handle things like this," Daphne assured the crowd of stunned students. She flashed her shiny badge to the crowd. A teacher fainted to the ground as the mouse let out an ear-shattering squeal and stomped its giant paws on the floor.

"Stay calm," the little girl said. "It's as afraid of you as you are of it."

All at once, every kid at Ferryport Landing Elementary freaked out. They screamed and ran toward every available exit. Some raced into classrooms, barricaded the doors with desks, and climbed out windows.

Puck peered into his pocket and smiled at Sabrina.

"Hang on, I've got a plan," he said, flashing her a grin. He spun around on his heels and transformed into an orange and white alley cat. Sabrina found herself clinging to the cat's ear as it charged toward the giant mouse. Once he got up close, Puck the cat hissed aggressively, but the mouse only stared down at him. Suddenly, what Sabrina could only describe as a smile crept across the mouse's face. It leaned its head down to the cat, opened its mouth, and roared angrily. Puck's short tabby hair was blown back as if he were standing in a heavy wind and Sabrina nearly flew off his ear. The cat backed away and transformed into a boy again.

"It was worth a try," Daphne shouted.

"Don't worry," Puck said, with Sabrina back inside his shirt pocket. "I've got a million more ideas where that one came from." The boy spun around to face the mouse and his wings popped out of his back. Flapping strongly, he soared over the mouse, spun around, and landed on its back.

"*Yee-haw!*" he cried, jabbing the heels of his feet into the mouse's side. The mouse squealed in pain, lifted itself on two legs, and kicked wildly, causing Puck to bounce around like a rodeo cowboy and Sabrina to be tossed around mercilessly inside the boy's pocket.

The giant mouse slammed into walls, broke down doors, and put serious dents into a row of lockers. It shattered a trophy case, sending glass, brass track medals, and bowling prizes skittering down the hallway. It crashed into a banner announcing the library's bake sale and ripped it off the wall.

Of course, Puck laughed at every effort the mouse made to buck him off. Sabrina suspected he'd ride the beast all day if it didn't get tired first.

"Puck, cut it out!" she shouted, clutching the top of the pocket, but she knew the boy couldn't hear her over the commotion he was making.

Daphne rushed across the hallway, avoiding the mouse's wicked flapping tail. She reached into her pocket and pulled out her half-full Drink Me juice box and aimed it at the mouse's mouth.

"Daphne, you're a genius!" Sabrina cried.

Daphne reached back like a big-league pitcher, waited for the mouse to open its gaping mouth, and tossed the juice box as hard as she could. Unfortunately, instead of slipping down the mouse's throat, the box bounced off one of the rodent's gnarly yellow teeth and fell to the ground. The mouse stomped down on the box, spraying the contents all over the hallway.

"Uh, what's plan B?" Wendell shouted, just as the mouse headed for the exit door. Unfortunately, Daphne was right in its path.

"Daphne, run!" Sabrina yelled, but there was no way the little girl could move that quickly. Luckily, Wendell raced across the hall and pushed Daphne to safety just as the enormous rodent lumbered past them like an out-of-control train. It slammed into the exit doors, knocking them off their hinges, and stomped outside.

Puck howled and laughed the whole way, until a low-hanging tree with a thick limb knocked him off the mouse. He fell hard on his back, sending his Drink Me box flying and launching Sabrina out of his pocket and onto the lawn several yards away. By the time Sabrina got her bearings, the mouse was already on top of the boy, doing what it could to sink its sharp teeth into him as Puck fought it off.

"Got any more of that juice?" he shouted, as Daphne and Wendell raced to his side. Puck snatched Wendell's Drink Me box with a free hand and squeezed its contents into the mouse's mouth until the box was crumpled and empty. Almost immediately, a ripple ran across the mouse's skin. The rodent shrank rapidly until it was once again a little brown mouse, sitting on the boy's chest.

Puck looked down at it and laughed. Then he ran his finger over the mouse's coat. "Good try," he told the rodent. "You almost had me."

Daphne helped Puck to his feet.

"Where's Sabrina?" she asked.

"Don't worry, marshmallow, she's right here in my pocket," Puck said as he looked inside. "Uh-oh."

"What's uh-oh?" Daphne cried.

"She's not in there," Puck said.

The little girl's eyes got as big as saucers.

"Don't anyone move," Wendell said. "She probably fell out here on the lawn and we could step on her."

"Sabrina!" Daphne shouted.

"I'm here!" Sabrina yelled, waving her hands and jumping up and down, but none of the children could see or hear her.

"What if we've already stepped on her?" her sister cried, as tears streamed down her face.

"Let's check," Wendell said. He slowly lifted each of his shoes. "She's not on mine."

Puck slowly looked under his sneakers. "All clear!"

Daphne checked one foot and then the next. A big smile came to her face.

"See, we haven't stepped on her," Wendell said.

"I think we better get the old lady," Puck said as his wings sprouted. "Best that I fly us out of here so we don't squish her."

In a few moments he had snatched the other children off the ground and they were all flying away.

"Don't you dare leave me out here!" Sabrina screamed, but they were already gone.

She looked around. The school was only steps away for a normal-sized person, but for her it seemed like half a mile. Staying put was probably the best idea, but the air was freezing even with her coat on, so she shoved her hands into her pockets and marched toward the entrance to the school.

When she finally reached the school's main doors, she found them in a heap—knocked off their hinges by the giant mouse—which left the hallway open to the bitter winter wind outside. Her walk had chilled her to the bone, and finding somewhere safe and warm to rest was now her main priority. She remembered that the heat in Mr. Sheepshank's office was always on full blast. If she was going to get warm, that was the place to go, so she ran down the hall, dodging a giant mound of discarded bubble gum, and made her way to the main office door. She'd hoped it would be a safe place to hide until Puck could return with her grandmother, but as soon as she crawled underneath the door she knew she had even bigger problems to deal with.

"There's another roach!" the secretary with the big glasses

cried. She reached into a drawer and pulled out an aerosol spray can, shook it vigorously, and got up from her desk. One glance at the can told Sabrina all she needed to know about what was going to happen next. It didn't take a rocket scientist to know what ROACH-BE-DEAD meant.

She ran along the rug frantically, racing under the secretary's desk just as the gigantic woman rounded the other side. This was unbelievable. A giant mouse had just been rampaging through the school and these goofy secretaries were worried about roaches? When Sabrina came into the light, the other secretary was there, chomping on a sandwich. She mumbled loudly and pointed at tiny Sabrina, causing the first secretary to come back around. The girl dashed under the desk again, but this time the secretary got down on her knees, pointed the spray can at her, and pushed the nozzle. Sabrina was sure she would soon be covered in a horrible poison and die, but luckily the nozzle was pointed upward and the chemical death landed all over the desk.

"This one's fast." The first secretary scowled.

"Don't send it running over here," the second secretary cried. "Those things give me the heebie-jeebies."

The first secretary raced around the desk just as Sabrina darted behind a file cabinet.

"Where did it go?" she groaned.

The second secretary had gone back to enjoying her sandwich and mumbled an "I don't know" to her coworker.

"I know where the filthy thing went," the first secretary cried. Suddenly, Sabrina's safe hiding place began to rock back and forth. The file cabinet moved several inches before it stopped. "It's heavy."

"I'm not a cockroach!" she shouted, but she knew the woman couldn't hear her. A stream of the poison came showering in from one side of the cabinet. Sabrina darted out of the way, but the secretary seemed to anticipate her escape route and was waiting for her on the other side. The girl looked up to find the nozzle of the can pointing right at her.

"Now I've got you," the woman cried.

But she never got her chance to spray the poison. Sabrina heard the office door open, and Mr. Sheepshank say, "Hello, ladies. The commotion is all over."

"What was it?" the secretary with the roach spray asked.

"Oh, just a big dog some kid let in," he replied. "Scared everybody half to death. Most of the kids have already left for home. Principal Hamelin just told me to let you two go, as well."

"Early dismissal for the grown-ups? I love it!" The roach-obsessed secretary cheered. She quickly forgot about Sabrina and crawled to her feet.

"I'm going home myself," the guidance counselor said.

Sabrina couldn't see what was going on, but she could hear the women packing their things and leaving. Sheepshank followed them out and closed the door.

After several minutes, Sabrina realized that the entire school was empty. All she could do now was wait, so she walked over to the desk of one of the secretaries and lay down under her big chair. The room was warm and comfy and before she knew it, she had fallen asleep.

• • •

Sabrina woke up inside Elvis's nose. Granny and Mr. Canis had used the big dog's excellent sniffer to track the tiny girl down, and when Elvis found her asleep under the chair, he accidentally inhaled her. With her head now covered in dog boogers and mucus, she kicked for freedom, but this only caused the dog to snort deeply, and Sabrina rocketed into his nasal cavity, slid down his throat, and was coughed out onto the floor.

When Sabrina got to her feet, Granny Relda was already standing next to her, holding two Eat Me cakes in her hand. She was as tiny as her granddaughter, but the anger on her face was as big as the moon. Her round face and button nose were so red with frustration Sabrina wondered if smoke might blow out of her ears.

"Granny, you won't believe what I found out," Sabrina said, hoping her news would change the old woman's mood.

"I agree, Sabrina," Granny Relda snapped. "I doubt I'll be believing anything you say for a very long time."

She handed the girl an Eat Me cake and quickly unwrapped her own. She took a big bite and began to grow. Sabrina ate her cake and felt her body sprout up, as well. Unfortunately, Elvis's boogers grew at the same rate and when she reached her normal size, even the Great Dane looked disgusted at the goo that covered her from head to toe.

Daphne, who was standing nearby, ran to hug her sister but halted when she saw the disgusting mess that covered Sabrina. "I'm sorry. I love you but you are way, way too gross," the little girl said.

"We got into the boiler room," Sabrina said, still hoping to impress her grandmother.

"She knows," Puck said sheepishly. He and Wendell leaned against the wall, looking guilty. Why wasn't everyone excited? They had found an important clue to the mystery.

"I also know you did it by breaking almost every one of my rules," Granny lectured. "Mirror says you have a set of keys for nearly three dozen of the rooms in the Hall of Wonders."

"I've been making copies," Sabrina said, lowering her eyes to the ground.

"How sneaky of you," Granny said. "I suppose you are proud of yourself?"

Sabrina knew it was not the right time to brag.

"You told us that this was our job," she argued. "Daphne and I didn't come banging on your door hoping that we'd get chased by giants and evil rabbits. Now that we're actually trying to take on this destiny of ours, you want us to stop."

"Sneaking around behind my back, defying my requests to stay out of this case, stealing and copying my keys, testing out magic and potions in the middle of the night, and dragging your sister into danger," said Granny. "Add that to your attitude about Everafters and I just don't see you as much of a help right now."

Sabrina's eyes welled with tears, but she refused to cry. She bit her lip hard and squeezed her fists tight. The last thing she would do was show the old woman that her words had stung.

• • •

Dinnertime was a quiet affair. No one talked, no one made eye contact, and no one smiled. Even Puck, who could usually be counted on to fart during dinner, was oddly quiet. When everyone had eaten, Granny quietly washed the dishes while Puck, Sabrina, and Daphne stared at one another from across the table. Elvis eyed Sabrina from time to time, but didn't seem to want to go near her after she had been inside his nose.

Just then, there was a knock at the door. Granny Relda stopped washing the dishes and rushed to open it. Snow White was standing outside in the cold. The old woman quickly invited her inside.

"Thank you so much for coming, Snow," she said as she took off her apron and folded it.

"I'm happy to help! Any chance to spend some time with my favorite student," the teacher said.

"That's me!" Daphne cried as she rushed to the door.

"Mr. Canis will be coming with me, and the sheriff is on his way now," Granny said. "The children have eaten, but feel free to raid the refrigerator. Hopefully, we won't be gone too long."

Just then, a car-horn blast came from outside.

"That's Hamstead," Mr. Canis said as he opened the closet and took out his and Granny Relda's coats.

"What's going on?" Sabrina asked.

"We're going to go and put a stop to what's going on under the school," Granny Relda replied. "While we're gone, Ms. White will be looking after you."

"You got us a baby-sitter?" Sabrina cried indignantly. "I'm too old for a baby-sitter."

"*You're* too old?" Puck said to her. "I'm over four thousand years old. This is an outrage!"

"I might have thought the same thing this morning," Granny replied as she put on her coat.

"*We* should go," Sabrina steamed. "We've seen the tunnels. We know how to get down into them."

There was another knock at the door. When Mr. Canis opened it, Wendell Hamelin stepped inside.

"Oh, we've got a guide," Granny replied.

"The sheriff says we better get going," the boy said, wiping his runny nose on his handkerchief. He looked more sad than excited about this latest detective assignment.

"Honey, you don't have to do this," Granny said. "This is your father we're going to arrest."

"Maybe I can convince him to stop before anyone else gets hurt," Wendell said. "He's my dad. I have to try."

Granny Relda, Mr. Canis, and Wendell, looking apologetically at the other three children, said their good-byes and were soon gone, leaving Sabrina standing by the door with a stunned expression.

"Well now," Snow White said uncomfortably, reaching into her handbag and pulling out a board game. "Who wants to play Candy Land?"

• • •

Snow White did her best to keep the kids busy. She set up the board game, but Puck had no patience for it. When he landed on Molasses Swamp and lost a turn, he flew into a rage, flinging the board out the front door and into the yard. Later, after he had calmed down, Ms. White suggested they play charades. Once again, Puck was the spoiler, acting out the names of tree gnomes and pixies that had lived three hundred years ago and insisting they were as famous as any astronaut or president. Eventually, even Snow White gave up and let the children do what they really wanted to do—research.

The girls searched the library for titles that might be of help. With half their family traipsing around in some dark tunnels, Sabrina and Daphne felt the least they could do was make sure that nothing had been overlooked. Sabrina eventually came across her great aunt Matilda's pamphlet entitled *Rumpelstiltskin's Secret Nature*. She could see it was going to be a dry read, so she fell into a chair and started on page one.

Rumpelstiltskin's story was a famous fairy tale; everyone had heard it, but Sabrina wasn't taking any chances with what she thought she knew. Dad's attitude about fairy tales had left the girls at a disadvantage, and she wanted to know the story inside and out. But even she was shocked to see how much information Matilda had collected about the little creature. It looked as if months of work had gone into the analysis of every single nuance of his personality, powers, and actions. Her ancestor even had theories on how Rumpelstiltskin spun wheat into gold, where he had come from, and why he tried to trick people out of their children.

Matilda's book also recounted at least two dozen versions of the original tale. The story Sabrina had always heard involved a woman who begged Rumpelstiltskin for his help. In exchange, she promised to give him her first-born child. When the baby finally arrived, the woman demanded a chance to keep it, so Rumpelstiltskin wagered that she would never be able to guess his real name. Of course, by the end of the story, she had figured it out and got to keep her kid, making the little man so angry he actually ripped himself in two. But Matilda said there was an alternate version of the ending that not many people knew. In the other ending, Rumpelstiltskin didn't rip himself in half—he actually blew up like a bomb, killing everyone within a mile.

One chapter, entitled "The Power of Rumpelstiltskin," contained theories on the source of the little man's powers. Matilda believed he was like a walking battery. He stored energy and converted it into destructive power. Unfortunately, the more of Matilda's theories Sabrina read, the more questions she had.

"It doesn't make any sense," Sabrina cried. "What do Rumpelstiltskin, the Pied Piper, the children of Everafters, and a bunch of tunnels under the school have in common?"

"The barrier," Puck replied.

"What?" Sabrina asked.

"The barrier runs very close to the school," Puck said. "We flew into it, don't you remember?"

"You're just telling me this now?" Sabrina cried.

"Seemed obvious to me," the Trickster replied.

"They're digging to the barrier," Snow White gasped. "Baba Yaga's spell is probably not as strong underground. But what would be the point? They'd still need a powerful magic explosion to get through it."

"I think they've got one," Sabrina said, holding up her great aunt's book. "Matilda thought Rumpelstiltskin was a walking nuclear bomb. He might be able to make a crack in it."

"Still, they have the river to worry about. The waters would drown them all," Snow White pointed out.

"Maybe not!" Daphne said, rushing to the bookshelf and snatching down one of the family's journals. She ran over to the table and put it down in front of Sabrina. It was their grandfather Basil's journal.

"Granny had this out one afternoon and forgot to put it

back," the little girl said. "I was flipping through it and found some maps Grandpa Basil drew of the town." She flipped it open and searched for a page. When she found it, she pointed for her sister to read.

Today I did a little amateur mapmaking of the elementary school construction site, claiming I was just interested in the building. Charming hates when he thinks I'm snooping, but I wanted to make sure no one got any ideas about digging the holes deeper or building a tunnel over to the river. The barrier is much weaker underground. Baba Yaga compensated though by extending it over the Hudson River. If anyone tried to tunnel through, they'd drown. The only chance they'd have would be to somehow dig through the bedrock under the river over to Bannerman's Island, but without an army of miners, they'd never get close. I feel pretty confident that it's impossible. —April, 1957

Sabrina flipped the page and found a hand-drawn map of the town and the surrounding areas. A circle enclosed the town and Grandpa Basil had written THE BARRIER on it as a label. She had to admit, the circle wasn't very big. Mount Taurus was inside it, as well as the edge of the Hudson River, but it wasn't a lot of room. She found the very spot where Puck had slammed into the barrier and dumped them all into the river. It was close to the school—as was a tiny island that sat right on the barrier. Sabrina had never noticed Bannerman's Island before, but there it was on her grandfather's map.

"Kids, let's just calm down," Snow White insisted. "Your grandfather was right. Without a crew of workers, it would take Rumpelstiltskin decades to tunnel to the barrier. Your grandmother and the sheriff will stop him and the piper tonight."

"See, that's where I'm confused," Sabrina said. "What does the Pied Piper have to offer in all this? If Rumpelstiltskin can blow a hole in the barrier, then what does he need with a guy whose claim to fame is leading a bunch of rats out of town?"

"Maybe he's using the rats to chew through the rocks," Puck said.

"That's stupid!" Sabrina snapped.

"You're stupid!" he shouted back.

"Maybe he's not using rats," Snow White said uncomfortably.

"What else could he use?" asked Sabrina.

"You don't know how the Pied Piper's story ended, do you?"

The girls shook their heads. Apparently, their father's no-fairy-tales rule was coming back to haunt them again.

"He drowned the rats and became a hero, right?" Daphne said.

"Well, he did drown the rats, but he didn't do it to be a hero. He did it for a paycheck. In his day, he used to travel from town to town, using his pipes to clean up messes. He drove the spiders out of Paris, the monkeys out of Bombay, and snakes out of Prague. But he did it for *money*. When he showed up in Hamelin, the townspeople were desperate. They were completely overrun with vermin."

"What's *vermin* mean?" Daphne asked.

"Rats and mice," Sabrina explained.

"Rats were everywhere," Ms. White continued. "They spread a lot of disease and people were getting sick. Everything the town had tried hadn't worked. So the piper agreed to handle their problem, and in no time he was leading the rats right into the ocean where they drowned. But that wasn't the end of the town's problems. When the piper came back, he wanted payment, but the town refused to pay. They had used him and he was furious."

"What happened?" Sabrina said, already sensing the story's unhappy ending.

"He gave them twenty-four hours to come up with the

money and when the time was up, they just laughed at him. So, he blew into his bagpipes and the town's children congregated around him. The piper marched out of town with the children following behind him, just as the rats had. Their families tried to stop them, but reports say the kids were in a trance and kept on following the music. The families never saw them again."

"So, of course it makes a lot of sense to hire him to be principal of an elementary school!" Sabrina said angrily.

"Rats or brats," Puck said, before Snow White could explain. "What's the difference?"

Suddenly, the truth dawned on Sabrina. "He's providing the workforce!" she cried.

"What are you talking about?" Daphne said.

"The piper has been using his magic to force the students to work at night. You've seen the kids in my classes. They're exhausted. It's because they've been working all night. We have to warn Granny!"

"We can't do that," Snow White said.

"But, Ms. White! We have to!" Daphne cried, rushing to the closet and returning with her deputy's hat tied to her head.

"The sheriff and Mr. Canis are with her," the teacher replied. "They'll figure this out before anyone gets hurt."

"What if they don't?" Puck asked. Sabrina was surprised. The boy usually acted as if he didn't care. "What if they don't find out? We saw those tunnels. They go on and on. If Rumpelstiltskin blows a hole in the barrier, those walls will collapse on everyone inside."

Now Sabrina was stunned. "I thought you were a villain. If you come along, you're going to have to be a hero."

"As long as I'm ruining someone's day I'm in," Puck said.

Snow White looked from child to child and then reached for her car keys.

"Get your coats on," she said. "But if I think it's too dangerous, we turn right around."

Soon they were rushing out the front door. They were in such a hurry, Snow White didn't see Mayor Charming coming up the path, and the two ran right into each other.

"Snow," Charming said, surprised.

"Billy," the teacher whispered.

They stood holding hands in the cold night air. Sabrina rolled her eyes.

"We're not going to go through this again, are we?" she cried. "We've got to get going."

"What's the rush?" Charming asked.

"Rumpelstiltskin and the Pied Piper have been tunneling under the school for months and are looking for the weak spot in Baba Yaga's barrier so they can try to crack a hole in it and escape, and Granny, the sheriff, Mr. Canis, and Wendell are there now trying to stop them, but they don't know that Rumpelstiltskin is like a living battery and he has the power to create the hole, but if he does he'll collapse the tunnel and everyone inside will die," Daphne said, breathing heavily.

Charming stood still with wide eyes. "What was that again?" he asked.

"We're going to save the day," Ms. White said.

"We'll take my car," the mayor declared, leading the group to his stretch limousine. Mr. Seven got out of the driver's seat, but Charming waved him off.

"Seven," he commanded. "We're in a hurry!"

The little man crawled back into his seat, closed the door, and started the engine. Once everyone was inside, he pulled into the road and sped off like a NASCAR driver, leaving a tire stain on the pavement behind him.

"Billy, what are you doing here?" Snow White said, as she strapped on her seat belt.

"I have something for the girls," the mayor explained as he reached into his pocket and took out a small box of matches.

Charming handed the box to Sabrina and smiled proudly. "We made a deal. Here's my end of the bargain."

"Uh, thanks," Sabrina said. "I'll save these for the next time I need to build a campfire."

"Child, those aren't ordinary matches!" Charming groaned. "They're the Little Match Girl's matches. I just handed you something people in this town would kill for."

Snow White gasped. "You told me they had been destroyed!"

"I was trying to protect you," Charming said. "If anyone knew these still existed, your life might have been in danger."

"Great, so you give them to us?" Sabrina groaned. "Doesn't everyone hate us enough?"

"Grimm, no one is going to know you have them, because you are going to use them right away," the mayor replied.

Sabrina peeked into the matchbox. Two small wooden matches lay inside. "What do they do?"

"I thought you two were supposed to be experts on fables and fairy tales. 'The Little Match Girl' is one of Hans Christian Andersen's most famous accounts."

"You've been in our house. There are like a million books in the bathroom alone. We don't know everything yet," Sabrina said.

"The Little Match Girl sold matches in the street for money," Snow White explained. "One day she came across a box of them and set out to make a little money to help feed her family. But it was horribly cold outside and she was forced to light one. The flame became a magical portal, leading to a room filled with food and a roaring fireplace. The girl realized she had just wished she were in such a place before striking the match. People have been looking for those matches for a hundred years. They'll take a person anywhere they want to go, Sabrina. All you have to do is wish."

"Like Dorothy's slippers?" Daphne asked. She and her sister had used them to pop up all over town, but they had lost one of them while running from a giant.

"These are more powerful than the slippers," Charming said. "They could take an Everafter to the other side of the barrier, or they could take you to your parents."

Sabrina stared down into the box and a tear rolled down her cheek. She didn't deserve such an amazing gift and she knew it. For weeks she had looked at every Everafter as a suspect in her parents' kidnapping. She had turned everyone against her and practically broken her grandmother's heart. And yet, here was the most obnoxious, untrustworthy of the bunch, handing her the key to finding her parents.

"Why would you do this for us?" Sabrina asked.

"We made a deal," Charming said, glancing at the pretty teacher.

"You could have used these to escape," said Snow White.

"There was something that kept me here," Charming said, staring into her eyes. The beautiful teacher leaned over and kissed the mayor. "Billy Charming, make me a promise."

"What kind of promise?" Charming asked, somewhat breathless.

"When all this is said and done," Snow White said, "Take me to dinner."

"As long as we can leave your seven chaperones at home," Charming said with a grin.

Mr. Seven grumbled in the front seat.

"Oh, it's so romantic," Daphne blubbered. "I think I'm going to cry!"

"I think I'm going to lose my lunch," Puck groaned.

Suddenly, the car came to a screeching halt.

"Seven, why have we stopped?" Charming demanded.

"The road is blocked, sir," the little man said, pointing out the window to where dozens of children were walking in the middle of the street. They were all wearing pajamas and had glassy looks in their eyes. "There are too many of them to maneuver around."

"The piper is controlling them," Sabrina said as they passed some of the kids.

Mr. Seven honked the horn, but it had no effect on the children.

"We'll have to walk from here," Sabrina said. They got out of the car, leaving Mr. Seven to guard it. Puck's wings sprang from his back and he lifted off the ground.

"What I wouldn't do for a carton of eggs," he said. "I'm going to go get some and play dive-bomber on these zombies."

Before he could fly away, Snow White grabbed his leg and yanked him back down to the ground. "We should stay together," she said. The boy looked extremely disappointed, but his wings disappeared nonetheless.

The group weaved in and out of the crowd until they were standing on the front lawn of the elementary school. As they approached the main entrance, Sabrina noticed that the front doors the giant mouse had plowed through were still lying on the ground. A steady stream of vacant-faced children were shuffling through the doorway, ushered in by a hulking girl with a pink ribbon in her hair. When Sabrina studied her closely, she realized that it was Natalie.

"Natalie, you need to get as far away from here as you can," she warned. "And try to get some of these kids to follow you. This place is going to get dangerous."

"Oh, it's going to get dangerous, all right," the big girl replied as her skin began to bubble and inflate. Hair shot from every pore and two long fangs sprang upward from her bottom jaw. Her eyes turned a milky yellow and a long hound-dog tongue crept out of her mouth and licked her lips. Claws sprouted from her fingertips as she lashed out at the group, knocking Puck, Charming, Daphne, and Sabrina to the ground with one great swipe. Snow White just managed to step aside, avoiding Natalie's attack.

"E-gad, I didn't think you could get any uglier," Puck said as he crawled back onto his feet.

"Snow, get behind me!" Charming shouted, as he leaped to his feet. "I'll handle this brute."

"Billy," the teacher cried. "This is the twenty-first century. Women don't need the white knight routine anymore. I can fight my own battles."

She planted her feet and raised her hands. When Natalie charged at her, the teacher sent a hard jab and a right hook into the beastie's face. The monster screamed angrily and lunged again, but this time, Snow White's foot came up and landed a hard blow to the monster's chest. Natalie tumbled to the ground, but sprang back to her feet, clawing and scratching at the pretty teacher. Ms. White blocked each blow with super-fast hands, until one of Natalie's punches actually connected and sent the teacher painfully to the ground. Instinctively, Charming and Puck stepped forward, ready to take over the fight, but Snow White flashed them an angry look.

"Gentlemen, please!" she said sternly. Charming and Puck threw up their hands in surrender and stepped aside. She sprang to her feet, planted them again, and then eyed the monster with a smile.

"Come and get it, ugly," she said. "School is in session."

Natalie roared and leaped at her. Snow White stopped the attack by jumping into the air, spinning around, and roundhousing the monster in the face. One of Natalie's fangs broke off in the middle and the monster fell to the ground, groaning in pain. The teacher stood over her with angry eyes and eager fists.

"If you were smart, you'd stay down," she said.

Sabrina and Daphne looked at each other in amazement.

"Snow, where did you learn to do all that?" Charming asked, obviously stunned by what he had just seen.

"I teach a self-defense class at the community center," Snow White replied. "We're called the *Bad Apples*. We meet every Saturday at four p.m."

"Sign me up," Daphne said.

"*Piper!*" Natalie shouted angrily as she crawled to her feet.

The principal stepped from out of the shadows. He was carrying a set of bagpipes and looked distraught.

"Do it!" the hairy girl raged.

"This has gone too far," Hamelin cried. "Let them save their grandmother and her friends. The barrier will still be broken and they won't pose a threat to you or your father again."

"Piper, I'll tell my daddy," Natalie threatened. "He's got your precious Wendell."

The principal raised his bagpipe's reed to his mouth and took a deep breath. "I'm sorry," he said to the group, and then he blew a long, sorrowful note into the air.

Everything went black.

10

"Sabrina! Wake up!" a voice shouted from far away. She tried very hard to pay attention to it but she was exhausted and dizzy. "Sabrina, you have to wake up now!"

She slowly opened her eyes. Mr. Hamelin was standing over her with a wild, desperate look on his face.

"What are you doing in my bedroom?" she grumbled.

"Sabrina, we're under the school!" Hamelin said, sounding frantic. "I know it's hard, but try to concentrate."

Sabrina looked around and saw she was standing in a huge tunnel, where children were rushing back and forth with wheelbarrows full of dirt and rubble. She looked down at herself and saw she was covered in soot and holding a shovel.

"Do you understand what has happened to you?" Hamelin asked.

"No," the girl replied. Her head felt heavy.

"I entranced you and your friends," the principal explained. "I had to. They have Wendell and they'll kill him if I don't do what they want."

"Where's my sister?" Sabrina demanded.

"They've got everyone—your sister, your grandmother, Canis, Charming, the sheriff, Snow, Puck, and my son—at the end of the tunnel. I managed to send you off into the mine to dig, and so far they haven't noticed."

"How long have I been down here?"

"Six hours."

"Six hours! They could all be dead."

"This is the soonest I could get to you," Hamelin said. "They've been watching me, but now that they've tunneled so close to the barrier, they don't seem to care that I ran off."

"Oh, I wouldn't say we don't care," a voice from behind them said.

Sabrina heard the sound of ripping flesh and Hamelin fell to the ground. The frog-girl was behind him, holding a bloody knife.

"You're coming with me," she hissed, grabbing Sabrina roughly by the arm.

Sabrina swung her shovel and hit the monster in the head so

hard the frog-girl fell to the ground and moaned. Sabrina rushed to help Hamelin.

"Wendell," Hamelin said, as blood pooled beneath him. "You have to find him and get him out of here."

"I'll come back for you," Sabrina said, and rushed into the nearest tunnel with her only weapon—the shovel—slung over her shoulder.

She scampered forward, stumbled over jagged rocks, and accidentally kicked over some abandoned tools. Dust lifted into the air and filled her lungs, choking her and making it that much harder to concentrate on where she was going. Each step was a challenge to her balance and, unfortunately, her path was a complicated, twisting, turning maze. Every few yards, she would spot a child she recognized from school. Each was glassy-eyed, staggering through the tunnels, hauling buckets of broken stones. None of them seemed to notice Sabrina pass them, even when she stopped and begged for directions. They were still under the piper's spell.

At last she spotted a faint light in the distance. As she came closer to it, the tunnel widened dramatically, revealing an enormous room carved out of the Ferryport Landing bedrock. She paused at the mouth of the room, doing her best to calm her breathing and listen for any movement. Hearing nothing, she lifted the heavy shovel off her shoulder and entered, swinging the weapon in the air in case anyone was about to ambush her. But she was alone. Only a few old buckets and a couple of tools littered the floor. There were no exits other than the way she had come. The tunnel was a dead end.

She raced back the other way, passing more of the zombie-faced, filth-covered kids. *I should head in the direction they're coming from,* Sabrina realized.

She darted down the tunnel, fighting the crowds of children. At one point, Natalie and the frog-girl came lumbering down the tunnel after her, but Sabrina stepped into the line of children, and being as filthy as they were, went unseen by the monsters. The tunnels went on and on. Some led to massive rooms, while others narrowed so that there was hardly room for two children to stand side by side, but eventually Sabrina found what appeared to be the end of the dig.

The room was high and wide and filled with boxes of dynamite and mining tools. A few flaming torches illuminated the room, but there were still deep shadows along the walls that Sabrina could not see into. Anyone could be hiding in one. She knew she was vulnerable.

"I've come for my family," she shouted into the cave. Her voice echoed off the stone walls and bounced around her ears.

Suddenly, something hit Sabrina squarely in the back. Unable to keep her footing, she tumbled over a sharp rock and fell hard onto her shoulder. Searing pain swam through her veins, followed by a dull, throbbing numbness. She tried to scamper to her feet, but her arm hung loosely at her side—it was broken. She cried out more in frustration than pain. But she grew quiet when she heard an odd clicking and hissing sound, followed by a disturbed laugh.

Using her good arm, she picked up the shovel that had slipped from her hand when she'd fallen and swung it around, doing her best to make it seem as if she had not been seriously injured. She walked in small circles, scanning the room for the source of the noise.

A long, spindly leg struck out from the shadows, narrowly missing her head. It slammed against the wall behind her, pulverizing stone into dust. Sabrina lifted the heavy shovel and swung wildly at the hairy leg, sinking its sharp edge deep into the monster's flesh. Shrieks of agony echoed through the cavern.

"I'm not going to be easy to kill," she threatened, hoping her voice sounded more confident to the monster than it did to her own ears.

"Kill you? This is a party!" the voice replied. One of the torches was snatched off the wall. It rose high into the air, shining its light on the ceiling. There, suspended in mounds of thick, horrible spiderweb, were her family and friends. "And you're the guest of honor."

Daphne, Granny Relda, Puck, Mr. Canis, Snow White, Sheriff Hamstead, and Mayor Charming hung above, with only their heads free of the sticky threads. Their mouths were covered as well, but Sabrina could hear Daphne's choked cries and Hamstead's angry groans and knew they were alive.

The spider monster slowly crawled out of the shadows and walked along the ceiling. It was gigantic and as Sabrina stared up at it, she realized that it wasn't simply a giant spider. The lower body was spider-like, but the upper body had the chest, head, and arms of a boy. Even with the two huge pincers that jutted from his mouth and clicked excitedly, she could tell it was Toby.

"Surprised?" Toby laughed.

"Not really," Sabrina admitted. "The bad guy is usually the ugly, giggling idiot."

"Then, I've got a surprise for you," a voice said from behind her. Sabrina spun around and found Natalie standing there. Sabrina noticed her front tooth was now missing. Then someone else stepped out of the shadows, someone who made Sabrina's heart ache—it was her only potential friend in the entire school—Bella. The blond girl put her arm around Natalie's shoulders and smirked.

"You're one of them, aren't you?" Sabrina said sadly. "Why did you pretend to be my friend?"

"Duh! She's evil," Toby said. He and the girls burst into laughter.

"You killed Mr. Grumpner," Sabrina gasped.

"Yes, I did," Toby said. "He was just too nosy and way too heavy with the homework."

"Don't forget Charlie," Bella said, patting Natalie on the back. "They just kept getting in the way of our father's plans."

Suddenly, the girl leaped into the air, higher than any human being could possibly leap. Even more startling, Bella's hands and feet stuck to the roof of the cave and her body started to change. Her skin looked as if it were filling with water. Dark spots rose to the surface on her hands and legs. Her eyes bugged out to disgusting proportions and migrated to the top of her head. Her shoes exploded off her feet, revealing long, green webbed toes. Within minutes, she had transformed into the frog-girl that had attacked the family and Principal Hamelin. Like a streak of lighting, a long, slippery tongue shot out of her mouth, latched onto Sabrina's shovel, and yanked it out of her hand.

When Sabrina turned, she saw Natalie had already made her transformation into the hairy animal she truly was.

"Rumpelstiltskin is insane," Sabrina said. "When he cracks a hole in the barrier, these tunnels will collapse and kill everyone in them. All the kids will die."

"Actually, the children are already outside, trying to figure out what has happened to them," a new voice said. Mr. Sheepshank emerged from the shadows.

"Mr. Sheepshank!" Sabrina cried. "You have to get out of here. They're going to blow this place sky high!"

"Duh, Sabrina," Toby the spider clicked. "You're even dumber than you seem in class."

"Hush, Toby," the counselor said. He turned to Sabrina. "They're not going to do anything of the sort. I'm going to do it."

"You're Rumpelstiltskin!" she gasped.

"Oh, I have many names," Sheepshank said. "But the one I like best is *Daddy*."

Sheepshank extended his arms and Natalie, Bella, and Toby rushed to stand by his side as the odd little man began to morph and bubble. But, unlike the others, Sheepshank didn't get bigger. In fact, he got a lot smaller. When his transformation was complete, he was hardly three feet high. His head, back, and arms were covered in kinky brown hair, but his face and pointed ears were pink like a pig's. He had a short, stubby tail, hoofed feet, and a couple of rows of sharp razor teeth.

"No fair," the little monster said sarcastically. "You guessed my name. Someone told you! Really child, I must agree with my son. You aren't as bright as your records suggest."

"Well, at least I'm not some sick pervert who steals children," Sabrina shouted, hoping to distract the little man and his freak show for a while longer.

"I don't steal children, Sabrina," the little creature said, as if he were genuinely insulted. "I care for them. These children have been treated with nothing but love and affection. I give them everything they ever wanted."

"Then what do you get out of it?" Sabrina asked.

"Why, I get their love, and their joy, and their sadness, and their frustration, and their hope, and most of all I get their anger," Rumpelstiltskin cackled. "I get their feelings, child, every last delicious morsel of them. You don't understand, do you? Let me spell it out for you. I feed on their emotions."

"That's where you get your power," Sabrina said, as Mr. Sheepshank's advice about feelings came flooding back to her. Of course he would encourage her to express her anger. He was eating it.

"You're starting to get it. That's the reason I have always loved

children. Their emotions are so raw and uncontrolled. When people get older, they've already found ways to control their feelings, but not children. Children are like emotional all-you-can-eat buffets. So, where's a guy with tastes like mine going to find work? Why, Ferryport Landing Elementary, of course! And trust me Sabrina, it has been a *truly* rewarding experience. For years, I sat back and feasted on the fights and humiliations you kids pile onto one another. The senseless bullying, the humiliation of being picked last for baseball, the endless teasing about someone's hair or clothes—when it comes to being mean, kids have cornered the market.

"Well, when the piper came to me with his plan to blow up the barrier from below, I was hesitant. After all, I had a pretty good thing going here at the school, and at night, well, I have these little rug rats to keep me fed."

The three Everafter children laughed at their "father's" teasing.

"But then I realized there's a great big world of anger, war, and pain for me to feast on out there. So, I signed on. It wasn't easy, though. Piper used his magic music, and every night the children of this school came to dig out the tunnels. At first, we tried to use all the kids, but the little ones are so weak, we had to make do with the fifth- and sixth-graders. Unfortunately, there was another unforeseen problem. The next morning, those same kids—the ones who supplied me with the most energy—were too sleepy to argue with one another. They went from a raging river of emotions to a dripping faucet overnight. The piper and I were just about to give up when you walked through the door."

"What do I have to do with it?" Sabrina asked, doing her best to buy time until she could come up with a plan.

"Sabrina, you're like the Niagara Falls of anger—it just keeps pouring over the edges. Every time you lost your temper, it was like a four-course meal with all the trimmings," Rumpelstiltskin said, as blue electricity crackled out of his fingertips.

"Once I tapped into it, I turned up the volume on you and could barely keep up with the energy," Rumpelstiltskin continued. "Truth be told, we probably didn't have to kill Grumpner or the janitor, but I could sense how outraged you would get. And it worked! Every little paranoia and prejudice was amplified by a million. Thanks to you, I finally have what it takes to blast a hole into the barrier. Once it's open, I'll be free and the Scarlet Hand will march across the world, destroying anyone who gets in their way."

"So, *you're* the Scarlet Hand," Sabrina said, even now feeling the anger rise within her. "You took my parents!"

"The Scarlet Hand isn't a person, child. It's a movement, an idea. It's bigger than all of us and I am just one spoke in a very big wheel."

"Where's my son?" a man shouted. Rumpelstiltskin shrieked and moved to safety behind Natalie's hulking body, just as Principal Hamelin raced into the cave. He looked exhausted, beaten, and on the edge of madness. His shirt was covered in his own blood and he limped painfully. In his hands were his bagpipes.

"Tell me where my boy is or I will play a song that will tear you apart," Hamelin raged as he charged at the little man. Rumpelstiltskin cowered in a corner.

"The boy got in the way," he cried, gnashing his teeth at his much taller partner. "I warned you about keeping him under control."

"Where is he?" Hamelin demanded.

Toby pointed one of his long, spindly legs at the ceiling. High on the cave wall, away from the others, was a mound of webbing from which no head poked and no movement came at all. Hamelin fell to his knees and buried his head in his hands.

"Bring him down, Toby," Rumpelstiltskin said.

"Awww, Dad, he was almost ready to eat," the spider kid whined.

"Do it," Rumpelstiltskin demanded.

Reluctantly, Toby scaled the wall, cut the web loose with his razor-sharp legs, and carried the boy gingerly to the ground. He set him down at Hamelin's feet and scurried back to his father.

"He was causing too many distractions," Rumpelstiltskin explained. "He was jeopardizing our plans."

Hamelin ignored the explanation as he tore the rest of the threads off his son. When the boy was finally free, Hamelin leaned down to listen for breathing.

"He's gone," Hamelin cried, as he set his boy down gently and climbed to his feet. He took his pipes and filled them with air. "And you are going to pay for it."

Before he could blow a single note, Bella leaped across the room, shot out her sticky tongue, and wrapped it around the bagpipes. She yanked the instrument out of the piper's hands and into her mouth, swallowing it whole.

"That's Daddy's little girl!" Rumpelstiltskin cheered.

Natalie rushed to a corner of the room and returned with a can. She dipped her hand inside it and when she pulled it out, it was covered in red paint. "Should I lay the mark on the kid's body?"

Hamelin shook with fury. "You and your Scarlet Hand, killing innocents. This wasn't part of our plan, troll! I just wanted out of this town."

"You've never had the backbone to do what has to be done, Piper," the little creature cried. "Someone had to make the hard decisions."

"Like killing my boy?" Hamelin said.

"I know your pain," Rumpelstiltskin said. "If I were to lose one of my children, I would be heartbroken, too. But I would still put them in harm's way for the greater good."

"These aren't your children!" Sabrina shouted. "You took advantage of their real parents. You played on their fears and made them feel hopeless. Their real parents want them back."

Toby looked confused. "Is that true, father?" the spider boy clicked. "You said they abandoned me in a park."

"They did, son," Rumpelstiltskin said.

"He's lying," Sabrina cried. "I've talked to your parents, Toby. They've been searching for you since the day they gave you to this sicko. He played with their emotions, made them believe you'd be better off with him. You weren't found in any park. Rumpelstiltskin manipulated your mom and dad and then paid them millions of dollars for you. He bought you, Toby, for the same reason he bought Natalie and Bella—so he could feed on you!"

"She's lying, children," Rumpelstiltskin said. "People are always lying about me! They want to take you away from me! It's not fair, children. Something has to be done to stop the people who hate me."

"We believe you, Father," Bella said, her face boiling with rage.

"Can we kill them now?" said Natalie as she looked at Sabrina with murderous eyes. Sabrina knew that Rumpelstiltskin could control the anger in others. Looking at the two girls, it was obvious to her that the little man had turned his power all the way up.

Rumpelstiltskin grinned. "How could Daddy resist his little Natalie? Go have your fun."

The monsters stalked Hamelin, backing him into a corner. Sabrina wanted to rush to his side, but Toby blocked her path. The Pied Piper was about to die and there was nothing anyone could do about it.

"Without your pipes you are nothing, Hamelin," Rumpelstiltskin said. "And now that the barrier has been reached, your usefulness has expired."

The piper reached into his pocket and pulled out something shiny. He looked down at it lovingly, then he raised it to his lips and blew into it. A low, sorrowful note came out of Wendell's harmonica and the ground began to shake violently.

"I don't need my pipes," Hamelin shouted at his former partner.

Suddenly, the floor cracked and a huge fissure opened. At first, nothing but steam belched out of it, but soon a flood of ants, worms, roaches, centipedes, and a million other creepy-crawling things flew out of the hole and attacked Rumpelstiltskin and his "children." The frog-girl leaped onto the ceiling, but was immediately overcome by a swarm of flying cockroaches. Losing her balance, she fell painfully to the ground.

Natalie was quickly overrun with centipedes that wiggled and raced along her body, biting her fiercely. The monster girl growled and whined, but soon fell to her knees, unable to fight.

Toby scurried around the cave, spraying webs at the sea of maggots that poured over him. He shrieked and cried as he rushed around the room, but the tide of insects was too much for him and he was engulfed.

Rumpelstiltskin didn't fare much better. Leaches covered the little man and he fell over in agony.

"Mr. Hamelin, please help me get to the roof," Sabrina said, grabbing her shovel. Hamelin blew into the harmonica again, and a rolling wave of spiders, worms, and roaches lifted Sabrina high off the ground to the ceiling above. Granny Relda was hanging closest, so Sabrina used her good arm to pull the cobwebs from the old woman's mouth and hands.

"Oh, *liebling*," Granny said. "This is one time I'm glad you didn't listen to my rules."

Sabrina smiled as she used her shovel to cut the sack of

threads from the wall. The wave of bugs expanded to hold the old woman up and when she was free she reached into her handbag and took out a pair of scissors. She put these into Sabrina's hand and then descended a flight of stairs the bugs created for her so she could easily step to the ground.

Sabrina rode the tide of creepy-crawlers to the next person, who happened to be Daphne. She yanked and pulled until the little girl was free, using the scissors to cut her off of the wall. Daphne was in tears, but she threw her arms around her older sister and hugged her tightly. The hug hurt Sabrina's arm, but she bit her lip and let her sister continue.

It was then that Sabrina noticed that Rumpelstiltskin was emitting a blue energy that swirled around him. A fireball blasted out of his chest, sending a huge explosion ripping through the caves, incinerating the entire insect army. The wave of bugs that supported Sabrina and Daphne turned to ash and the two girls tumbled to the ground, jarring Sabrina's broken arm and causing an agony that nearly knocked her unconscious. Through the haze of pain, she saw that the blast had destroyed some of the cave tunnel and sent tons of rock tumbling to the ground, blocking the only exit. Worse still, the blast had damaged the foundation of the cave and large chunks had begun to fall from the ceiling.

"Look what you have done!" Rumpelstiltskin shrieked. He

lunged at the principal and knocked him down. In the struggle, Hamelin's harmonica slipped from his hand and slid across the cave floor, and was crushed by a falling boulder.

While the two Everafters fought, Granny Relda said, "Girls, we have to find a way to get the others down."

"I have an idea," Daphne replied. She took Granny Relda's scissors and shoved them into her pocket, then rushed over to the unconscious frog-girl. She kneeled down and rubbed her hands all over the beast's super-sticky skin. Then she rubbed her sneakers until they were covered in the goo, as well. Then she rushed to the wall, pressed her hands against the stone, and slowly but effortlessly climbed the wall. Each step made a squishy sound.

"*Liebling*, do be careful," Granny Relda cried.

"That is so punk rock!" Sabrina shouted.

When the little girl got to where Puck was trapped, she used the scissors to cut through the spider's web. Soon Puck was free and as indignant as ever. He sprouted his wings and fluttered around the room.

"Someone is going to pay for this," he shouted.

Meanwhile, Daphne went to work on Snow White. As soon as the teacher was free, Puck carried her back down to the ground safely. Soon, he was doing the same for Mayor Charming and then Sheriff Hamstead. Daphne crawled along the ceiling to the last of their group, Mr. Canis, but before she could even cut away a strand, she slipped and fell. Puck caught her just before she hit the ground.

"I ran out of sticky stuff," Daphne said.

In the meantime, Hamelin had picked up the gnashing Rumpelstiltskin and thrown him violently against a wall. The little man slumped to the ground and lay very still. The piper rushed back to cradle his son. Snow White followed and crouched beside him.

"It's too late," Hamelin whimpered.

"No, it's not," the pretty teacher replied as she felt Wendell's wrist. "He's got a pulse." Snow White took the boy, laid him flat on his back, and tilted his head up. Then she took a deep breath and blew it down the boy's throat. Instantly, Wendell shuddered and coughed. He was alive!

"He had some of the cobwebs in his throat," the teacher said. "He couldn't get any air."

Hamelin stroked and kissed Wendell on the forehead.

"Dad," the boy said, "I think I solved the mystery."

Hamelin laughed and sobbed at the same time. "I know you did, son! You're a great detective!"

"Thank you! Thank you for saving my son!" the principal cried. He reached over and gave Snow White a huge kiss on the mouth. Charming was standing nearby and raised his eyebrows as Snow White blushed. Then he scowled.

Rumpelstiltskin crawled to his feet. He looked at his fallen children and a tear rolled down his face.

"It's over," Sabrina said.

"Oh, it's far from over," Rumpelstiltskin said. "All I need to do is collect some more power, and there's someone in this room that could give me enough to blow this little town off the map."

Sabrina had never been afraid of anything the way she was of this little man. He knew her anger, he feasted on it, and she had provided him with enough raw energy to destroy them all. But she wasn't going to let him play with her head any longer.

"You can't do it," she said. "I'm not angry anymore."

"True," the little man replied. "I'll miss your rage. It was delicious. But I'm not talking about you, child. I'm talking about the Wolf."

Sabrina gazed up at the skinny old man still trapped in his web prison. Even from such a distance, she could see the fear in Mr. Canis's eyes. It was the first time she had ever seen the old man afraid of anything. It seemed to unsettle Charming, as well, because the prince stepped in front of Rumpelstiltskin with his fists clenched.

"We're trapped down here, troll," Charming said. "If you pull that stupid trick of yours on the Wolf, you'll let him out, and he'll kill us all."

"No, my friend, he will save us all," Rumpelstiltskin said. "The Wolf will bring the barrier down, freeing us from this prison! Freeing himself from his own prison, as well. Look at him— trapped inside Canis, parading around like he's human! He's just like us, except his barrier is his own body. It's disgusting! We're Everafters. We shouldn't be acting like humans, we should be ruling over them. The Wolf will be thrilled to help. His rage will open the barrier and the world will be ours for the taking!"

Sabrina watched Mr. Canis struggle, but the change was already coming on him. The webs ripped as the old man's body tripled in size. A hideous roar echoed over the crumbling walls and the Wolf was free. He fell to the ground, sending a shockwave through the floor as he landed on his feet. He looked around at the desperate group and licked his lips.

"Guess who's back!" he snarled as he struck Charming, throwing him against a wall. The Wolf sniffed the air. "What's for dinner? Something smells good!"

Puck's wings sprang from his back and he stepped in front of the Wolf.

"What's this? An appetizer?" the beast asked. "Relda, you sure do put on a fancy party."

"You know me, Wolf," Puck said bravely. "You take another step or try to harm anyone here and you will have to answer to me."

The beast studied the boy for a long moment and then a chuckle came up through his throat. "Trickster," he said, sniffing the boy. "Love will be the end of you."

Puck blushed. "I don't know what you're talking about."

The Wolf turned and eyed Sabrina. He chuckled and then turned his eyes back on the boy.

"All right, hero. I'm going to make you famous," the Wolf growled.

The boy spun around on his feet and immediately transformed into an elephant. He snatched the Wolf up in his long trunk and smashed him against the wall. The Wolf fell to the floor, stunned.

"Fantastic!" Rumpelstiltskin cried out. A glimmer of the blue energy began to swirl around him.

"Puck, stop!" Sabrina cried out, but Puck was still in the moment. He transformed back into his true form and drew his wooden sword. He jammed it into the beast's belly and the Wolf winced. Puck couldn't know he was actually helping Rumpelstiltskin build the Wolf's rage.

"Stay down, dog," the boy shouted, smacking the Wolf on the top of the head with his sword. "Or there'll be no table scraps for you."

The beast opened his big blue eyes and laughed. "You're a funny boy!" He sprang to his feet so quickly that Puck nearly fell backward. The boy's wings erupted from his back and he flew into the air, hovering at the top of the cave. The Wolf leaped high, grabbing at the boy with his claws, missing him by only inches.

Puck laughed and stung the beast's paws with his sword. If it hurt, the Wolf didn't seem to mind. His face was a combination of anger and amusement. It was horrifying to watch. Luckily, Puck seemed to be out of his reach, until the boy's wing clipped the ceiling and he fell to the ground. The beast lunged at the boy, grabbed him in his huge claws, and opened his jaws wide. His fangs glistened in the tunnel light.

Suddenly, Daphne was standing in front of him.

"Stop it right now!" she demanded.

The Wolf turned to look at the little girl with sadistic amusement. "Don't worry, child," the Wolf said. "You'll get your turn to fight for your life."

"Daphne!" Granny cried.

"Leave Puck alone," Daphne said. "And let me talk to Mr. Canis."

The Wolf snarled. "Child, Mr. Canis is not real. There is only me."

"I know that's a lie!" the little girl cried. If she was afraid, Sabrina couldn't see it. "Mr. Canis is real because I said he is. He's part of my family and I love him!"

Briefly, the Wolf's face changed. For a flickering moment, Sabrina saw his steel-blue eyes change to Mr. Canis's dull gray ones. The old man was inside, trying to control himself.

"Daphne," the Wolf said quietly, dropping Puck. Then a shudder ran through him and any trace of their family friend was buried again. His disorientation gave Puck another opportunity to attack. The boy climbed to his feet and picked up a large rock from the ground. He tossed it as hard as he could, beaming the beast in the head.

"Hey, Wolf, you ever hear of a game called dodgeball?" he said.

"Death is moments away for you and you want to discuss a child's game?" The Wolf laughed.

Puck threw the boulder and it hit the Wolf in the chest, knocking the air out of the big brute.

"I don't want to talk about it," he shouted, bending over for another boulder. "I want to play it!" With impossible speed, he tossed one heavy rock after another at the beast.

"Puck! *Stop!*" Sabrina shouted.

The boy looked over at her. His face was red with excitement, but his eyes were full of confusion.

"Uh, I'm trying to save your life, Grimm," the boy said.

"You're going to kill us all," Sabrina said. "You're making Rumpelstiltskin stronger."

The Wolf staggered to his feet. "No child, you've got it wrong. I'm going to kill you all."

"Take a look around you, rover," Snow White said, stepping between the Wolf and Sabrina. "Your little tantrum is helping to fuel your destruction."

The Wolf turned to face the beautiful teacher. She continued, "The angrier you get the stronger the real enemy becomes." She pointed at Rumpelstiltskin, who was encircled in his blue energy. He seemed to be enjoying each second of the fight. The Wolf turned to face the little creature and immediately the blue glow around him expanded.

"What are you up to, little man?" the beast growled.

"Fantastic," Rumpelstiltskin cried. "Your rage is unbelievable."

"He's powering himself with your anger and when he has enough he's going to blow up this cave and bury everyone in it, including you," Granny Relda chimed in.

"You're signing your own death warrant!" Hamelin added. He had managed to get Wendell to his feet, but the boy was dizzy and obviously needed a doctor.

"Keep going, people," Rumpelstiltskin shouted. "Direct his anger at me!"

"You *want* my rage?" the Wolf said.

"It's fantastic," the creature said.

The Wolf eyed Sabrina closely. He had an odd expression on his face, filled with disgust and disbelief, one that seemed to say, *Can you believe this guy?* If Sabrina hadn't been so terrified, she might have laughed, but she did recognize the opportunity. The Wolf's attention was no longer on eating everyone in the room. He wanted a fight.

Sabrina cocked an eyebrow at the Wolf and said, "Sick 'em, boy!"

The Wolf turned on Rumpelstiltskin and lunged forward, grabbing the little creature. As soon as they collided, both were enveloped in the blue energy.

Sabrina's arm hurt so much she tried to prop it up with her knee. It brushed against a lump in her pocket. The little matchbox! Her eyes lit up as she pulled it out. Inside were the two matches. She removed one, wished she were outside, and struck the match. In the flame, she could see the outside of the school. Everywhere, dirty students milled around in confusion, having just broken free from the piper's magic.

"Sabrina, where did you get those?" Granny Relda asked.

"Charming. We need to get everyone out of here!" Sabrina shouted over the fighting. She tossed the match on the floor and a giant flame appeared.

"Mr. Hamelin," Sabrina shouted, "get Wendell out of here!" Hamelin nodded, picked up his son, and stepped into the flame. Daphne and Granny rushed to Toby, and together they dragged the big spider by his legs through the portal. As they did, Sabrina heard the old woman ask Puck to help with the other Everafter children. He spun around on his heels and transformed into a gorilla, hoisted Bella and Natalie onto his back, then raced through the flames himself. Snow White and Sheriff Hamstead helped the mayor to his feet and together they raced to the portal.

"*I'm* supposed to rescue *you*," Charming said to Snow White.

"Maybe it's time we both started trying some new things," Snow White said as the three disappeared into the flames.

Granny came back through the portal and waited for Sabrina.

"We can't leave him down here," Sabrina cried, as she watched the Wolf and Rumpelstiltskin fighting.

"I believe Mr. Canis knows what he is doing," Granny Relda said.

"I won't go," Sabrina insisted, but Granny grabbed her sweater and dragged her through the portal. In a flash, they were standing outside in the cold, with a hundred elementary school students, who were staring at the gorilla carrying a big, hairy girl and a frog monster.

"This is going to take a lot of forgetful dust!" Daphne said, under her breath.

"Get away from the school!" Sabrina shouted to the children and they obeyed. They ran for the parking lot just as Sabrina heard a slow, horrible rumble from below. Everyone raced to the other side of the road, where some children were already congregated. When she reached them, Sabrina turned and watched the school. The horror unreeled like a car crash you couldn't stop watching. First, smoke billowed out of the school's windows, then a terrible explosion blew out the glass and knocked the doors off their hinges. The roof collapsed, a flame a hundred feet high shot out of the center, and then the ground around it sank and the school fell into it. Finally, a cloud of dust rose up, covering the site, and when it settled again, the school was gone. Only a huge hole remained as evidence that there had been anything there at all.

"Mr. Canis," Sabrina gasped. "He's gone. I killed him."

"Sabrina, don't," Granny pleaded.

"This is all my fault!" the girl said as she broke down in tears.

"No, child, you arc not responsible for this." Granny tried to reassure her. Sabrina pulled away.

"It was my anger and my prejudice that did this," she cried.

"Child, Rumpelstiltskin manipulated you," her grandmother insisted.

"He only manipulated what was already inside of me."

"Oh, *liebling*."

Suddenly, Beauty and the Beast, the Frog Prince and his Princess, and Little Miss Muffet (aka Mrs. Arachnid) and the spider raced through the crowd of children.

"We heard there was trouble at the school," the Beast grunted. "Have you found our kids?"

Puck pointed at the three unconscious monsters lying on the ground. The parents cried out in unison and rushed to their children. The Beast picked up his grotesque, unconscious daughter, Natalie, and lifted her into the air. "She's beautiful, darling," he cried to his wife.

Sabrina watched the happiness in the parents' eyes. The Frog Prince and his wife kneeled down to their unconscious daughter, Bella, and slowly caressed her face. Even the spider cooed over his son, Toby. They loved their monstrous, murderous children. Sabrina looked into her box of matches. She reached in and took out the last of the Match Girl's matches. She could save it until her arm was well, then rescue her mom and dad, but it would take weeks. She couldn't be without them for another day. She needed them right now. She made a wish, then struck the match against the box's flinty surface. The flame came to life and shined in the cold night.

"Sabrina, no!" Granny Relda cried.

"Look at what I've become," the girl said sadly. "I need my mom and dad."

"Sabrina, you listen to me! I forbid it. It's too dangerous," Granny said, but Sabrina could already see her parents, safe and asleep on a bed, inside the flame. She tossed the match to the ground and the portal grew. Without even a glance at her grandmother or sister, she stepped through and found herself on the other side.

The room was dark. It was also warm, which made Sabrina a bit dizzy, stepping from such icy cold air into the heat. She shook off the dizziness and rushed to her parents, embracing them both the best she could.

"I'm going to take you home, now," she said, dragging her unconscious mother from the bed and onto the floor. She pulled as strongly as she could with her one good arm, edging closer and closer to the portal, where she could see Granny, Daphne, and Puck waiting with worried faces.

Suddenly, Daphne's face grimaced in terror and she started shouting, but Sabrina couldn't hear a word. Sound didn't cross the portal.

What is she trying to tell me?

And that's when the figure stepped out of the shadows. Sabrina knew she might someday have to confront her parents' kidnapper, but her imagination had not prepared her for the person she now saw in front of her. She was a child, probably Daphne's age, wearing a red cloak and a sadistic grin. Sabrina had never seen an expression like that on a little girl.

"Did you bring my puppy?" the child asked, sniffing the air.

"Who are you?" Sabrina asked.

"No, you didn't," the little girl said angrily. "But you've been around my puppy. Where is he?"

The little girl reached out and put her hand on Sabrina's shirt. When she removed it, a bloodred stain remained—a handprint.

"I can't play house without my grandma or my puppy," the girl said.

"I don't know what you're talking about," Sabrina said, trying to find the strength to get her mother through the portal.

"Yes, gibberish, that's what I speak," the little girl agreed. "Not a word makes sense. That's what they said. They said I had imagination."

"What do you want?"

"I want to play house!" The little girl's face grew very angry and she pointed a finger at Sabrina.

"I have a mommy and a daddy and a baby brother and a kitty. Do you want to pet the kitty?"

Just then, Sabrina heard an inhuman voice slurping and slavering behind her. It said, "Jabberwocky, Jabberwocky, Jabberwocky" over and over again. She turned to see what was making the noise and a shriek flew out of her throat. Hunching over her was something too impossible to exist—a combination of skin and scales and jagged teeth. Even in a town like Ferryport Landing, Sabrina had never seen some-thing that brought so much horror.

"My, you are an ugly one," a voice said from across the room. The monster turned. Puck was standing next to the portal, hands on hips, like some kind of comic-book hero. "Come on, Grimm. I'm here to rescue you."

With a hiss, the portal burned out and closed behind him. Puck looked back and grimaced. "Uh-oh."

The little girl screamed with rage. *"I don't need a sister or another brother! I need a grandma and a puppy!"*

Suddenly, the monster swung its enormous arm at Sabrina, and then the room went black.

To be continued . . .

ABOUT THE AUTHOR

Michael Buckley is the *New York Times* bestselling author of the *Sisters Grimm* and *NERDS* series. He has also written and developed television shows for many networks. Michael lives in Brooklyn, New York, with his wife, Alison, and his son, Finn.

This book was designed by Jay Colvin and art directed by Becky Terhune. It is set in Adobe Garamond, a typeface that is based on those created in the sixteenth century by Claude Garamond. Garamond modeled his typefaces on those created by Venetian printers at the end of the fifteenth century. The modern version used in this book was designed by Robert Slimbach, who studied Garamond's historic typefaces at the Plantin-Moretus Museum in Antwerp, Belgium.

The capital letters at the beginning of each chapter are set in Daylilies, designed by Judith Sutcliffe. She created the typeface by decorating Goudy Old Style capitals with lilies.

A GUIDE TO FAIRY TALES
& THE SISTERS GRIMM

Dear Reader,

When I set out to write the adventures of the Sisters Grimm, I wanted to update everyone's favorite fairy-tale characters using adventure, humor, and surprises. I thought it would be easy. After all, I had heard all the stories and seen all the movies. What else was there to know?

It turns out there was plenty more to know.

When I reread some of the original stories, I found that everything I thought I knew was wrong. Imagine my surprise when I discovered that the Little Mermaid didn't win her handsome prince's heart in the end. Or that Pinocchio wasn't swallowed by a whale but eaten by a shark! Or that Snow White wasn't awakened with a kiss but when the piece of poisoned apple, stuck in her throat, was dislodged. I went back and reread all the classics, by the Brothers Grimm, Hans Christian Andersen, Lewis Carroll, Andrew Lang, Rudyard Kipling, L. Frank Baum, and dozens more. What I found was a wealth of funny, exciting, scary, and adventure-filled stories, and my hope is that the Sisters Grimm series will inspire you to do the same. Your local library should have a wide collection of fairy tales and folklore, filled with as many surprises as there are in Sabrina and Daphne's adventures. I invite you to crack open these classics and find out what you've been missing. Happy reading and beware of the Scarlet Hand!

—Michael Buckley

Fairy Tales

Many people think fairy tales are just stories about princesses and witches that our parents tell us so we won't take candy from strangers or wander off by ourselves. But if fairy tales were only here to teach us lessons, they probably would have disappeared long ago.

Fairy tales tell us big truths about life, not just as it was long ago, but as it is today, and show us how to make our way through it with bravery, cunning, and wisdom. They are such useful guides that they've been followed for centuries, by people in every country on the globe. Two hundred years ago, a young girl fell asleep in her bed listening to the same fairy tale you liked to read when you were little.

So how did fairy tales from so long ago end up here? For a long time, fairy tales were only passed down orally. That means, basically, that they were created from a giant, centuries-long game of telephone. People told stories to children, friends, or strangers they met during their travels. Then those people told the stories to other people, changing little details along the way. The general plots stayed the same, but the stories grew and changed, depending on where and when they were told. Sometimes two different versions of the same story would pop up in two different countries. The names and settings would be different, but the same things would happen. For example, there are versions of the Cinderella story in countries as far apart as Egypt and Iceland!

Following Fairy Tales. The Cinderella story is one of the most famous fairy tales in the world because it's been adapted to so many different cultures and times. The first written version appeared more than a thousand years ago in China, and new versions of the tale pop up all the time—think of all the movies you've seen about a poor, mistreated girl who ends up with the rich, handsome guy. The details change—maybe "Cinderella" works in a car wash or ropes cows—but the plot stays the same.

You can conduct your own experiment to see how fairy tales might grow or change. All you'll need is a piece of paper, a pen, and a few friends.

Have one person start writing two or three sentences on the paper to begin the Cinderella story. Then have that person fold the paper down, so only the last line he or she wrote can be seen.

Pass the paper on to the next person, who will add a few sentences to the story, with only the line before as a guide. Then the second writer should fold the paper again, so that only the last line of his or her writing is visible. Continue to pass the paper, write, and fold until you finish a page, or two if you're feeling ambitious. When you're done, unfold the paper and read the whole story through. See if you can trace how the storyline and characters changed as the story was passed from one person to another.

GRIMMS TO THE RESCUE

For a long time, people told fairy tales by memory, and often stories were changed or even lost as they were passed down. That's when the Brothers Grimm stepped in. Jacob and Wilhelm Grimm grew up in Germany listening to fairy tales, and they worried that the wonderful stories they heard might be changed, lost, or forgotten. The brothers decided to write down their favorite tales so people would remember them forever. Some people think of the Grimm brothers as writers, and they were, but more than writers they were collectors—even hunters—of good stories. They talked to everyone, from their close friends to strangers they met traveling. Once, they met a poor, ragged soldier who asked for their old clothes in exchange for his stories. The Brothers Grimm were more than happy to make the trade—in fact, they probably thought they were getting the better deal!

You may have heard different versions of the same fairy tale, some scarier than others. When the Grimm brothers first wrote their stories down, they were violent tales, packed with villains who died in horrible ways. The Grimms thought that adults, especially professors and historians, would be the ones reading their stories. They were surprised when they realized that it was kids who liked their fairy tales best! So Wilhelm and Jacob rewrote their stories, making them more poetic and a little less violent. But they didn't take everything out, because they knew that being scared was part of the fun of reading fairy tales. They didn't want to cheat their younger readers of a good story.

THE BASIC INGREDIENTS

It seems that an awful lot of fairy tales are full of wicked witches, endangered princesses, and handsome princes who save the day. That's because putting together a fairy tale is kind of like putting together a potion, and different stories use many of the same ingredients. What does a good fairy tale need? Here's a list of some of the most common elements of fairy tales:

Heroes/good characters
Villains/very, very bad characters
Interesting sidekicks
A journey or quest
Magic
A happy ending

Can you think of any other important components of a good fairy tale?

Do you think all of these components are necessary to a good story?

Some fairy tales, like many of the stories written by Hans Christian Andersen, don't end happily. Others, like some more modern renditions of old fairy tales, don't include magic.

As you read *The Sisters Grimm*, look for elements from the list above and see how many you can find. Think of Sabrina, Daphne, and Granny Relda as heroes (or "damsels in distress," sometimes). Who are the villains? Do you ever feel sorry for them? Think about different ways in which *The Sisters Grimm* imitates or challenges the typical fairy-tale formula.

CRIME WATCH

The Grimm sisters are "sleuths of fairy-tale crime." It's a good thing, too, because there seem to be an awful lot of crimes committed in fairy tales. Without the three little (or not so little) pigs out patrolling the streets, crime was rampant throughout many classic fairy tales. Below are some well-known fairy tales and a list of crimes. Can you connect the crime with the story, and bring the perpetrators to justice like the Grimm sisters?

Goldilocks	A	1	Lying
Little Red Riding Hood	B	2	Identity theft
Beauty and the Beast	C	3	Destruction of property
Snow White	D	4	Child labor
Rumplestiltskin	E	5	Hostage-taking
Cinderella	F	6	Attempted murder
The Three Little Pigs	G	7	Breaking and entering

Answers:

A-7 (Goldilocks enters the house of the three bears uninvited)

B-2 (the wolf pretends to be Grandma)

C-5 (the beast makes Beauty stay in his castle and will not let her leave)

D-6 (the evil queen tries to kill Snow White four times)

E-1 (the girl's father lies and tells the king that she can spin gold out of straw)

F-4 (the evil stepmother and her daughters make young Cinderella their slave)

G-3 (the wolf destroys the pigs' houses)

Be the Next Grimm

Not everybody may get the chance to hang out with Everafters and solve fairy-tale crimes like the Grimm sisters, but anyone can follow in the Grimm brothers' famous storytelling tradition. Because most fairy tales follow a pretty simple formula, it's surprisingly easy to create your own. See if you can use some common building blocks to write your own story. Here are a few questions to get you started thinking:

Who is the hero?

Who is the villain?

Is there a trusty sidekick?

Where does my story take place?

What does my hero want? What is he or she looking for?

What challenges must my hero overcome?

Once you decide what you're writing about, here are some phrases to help you put your ideas all together:

Once upon a time . . .

There once was a boy . . .

Many, many years ago there lived . . .

Now, you shall hear a story that somebody's great-great-grandmother told a little girl many years ago . . .

. . . and _____ was in grave danger . . .

. . . but _____ was too smart to be tricked, and decided to . . .

. . . and they lived happily ever after!

. . . snip, snap, snout. This tale's told out.

Remember, part of the fun of fairy tales is being surprised, so be as creative as you can. Boys don't always have to rescue girls, and villains don't always have to be wicked old women (think about the surprising heroes and villains in the Sisters Grimm books). After you finish your fairy tale, try reading it out loud to see how it sounds. You'll be working in the great, centuries-old tradition of Jacob and Wilhelm Grimm!

Test Your Fairy-Tale Smarts

Think you have the smarts to be part of the Grimm family? As Granny Relda teaches, there's lots to learn. See how much you know by taking the following quiz about your favorite tales!

1. The seven dwarfs make an agreement with Snow White allowing her to stay with them if in return she will do what?

a. stand around looking pretty

b. teach them how to wash all the dust off their mining clothes

c. cook, clean, and keep house

d. accompany them to the mines every day and sing while they work.

2. At the very end of Little Red Riding Hood, the wolf's stomach is filled with
   a. Granny's famous chicken wings
   b. Granny
   c. absolutely nothing
   d. stones

3. Before the Queen guesses Rumplestiltskin's real name, she guesses two others, including
   a. Harry
   b. Joshua
   c. Jack
   d. Prince Charming

4. The Evil Sorceress who finds Hansel and Gretel plans to
   a. feed them her leftovers forever
   b. make them clean her house all day long
   c. hold them hostage until their parents pay for them
   d. eat them

5. Rapunzel is raised by an evil enchantress to punish her parents for
   a. exiling the enchantress from their kingdom
   b. stealing some plants from the enchantress's garden
   c. having the fairest daughter in all the land
   d. not taking their daughter to get a haircut when she clearly needs one

Answers: 1-c, 2-d, 3-a, 4-d, 5-b

Original Tales

If you are curious about the original stories collected by the Brothers Grimm and other storytellers from around the world, here's a list of books to start you off, which you should be able to find at your local library:

Andersen's Fairy Tales. Hans Christian Andersen. Wildside Press, 2004.

The Annotated Classic Fairy Tales. Norton, 2002.

The Arabian Nights Entertainments. Andrew Lang. Dover, 1969.

Celtic Folk and Fairy Tales. Joseph Jacobs. Dover, 1968.

Chinese Myths and Fantasies. Cyril Birch. Oxford, 1993.

The Complete Fables. Aesop. Penguin, 1998.

The Complete Fairy Tales of Charles Perrault. Charles Perrault. Clarion, 1993.

The Complete Grimm's Fairy Tales. The Brothers Grimm. Pantheon, 1976.

Demons, Gods, and Holy Men from Indian Myth and Legend. Shahrukh Husain. Schocken, 1987.

English Fairy Tales. Joseph Jacobs. Everyman's Library, 1993.

The Fairy Books. Andrew Lang. Various publishers.

Greek Gods and Heroes. Alice Low. Simon & Schuster, 1985.

Irish Fairy Tales and Legends. Una Leavy. O'Brian Press, 2002.

Italian Folk Tales. Italo Calvino. Harcourt, 1990.

Russian Fairy Tales. Aleksandr A. Afanasiev. Pantheon, 1976.

Spirits, Heroes, and Hunters from North American Indian Mythology. Marion Wood. Knopf, 1982.

Tales of Ancient Egypt. Roger Lancelyn Green. Puffin, 1996.

The Grimm Web

You can find out more about the Brothers Grimm and their stories at these Internet sites:

Brothers Grimm: Fairy Tales, History, Facts, and More

www.nationalgeographic.com/grimm

National Geographic presents twelve tales from the famous brothers in their original form. Open the treasure chest to find a map of the Fairy-Tale Road through Germany, *National Geographic* articles on the Brothers Grimm, links to other Grimm resources, and more.

Grimm Fairy Tales

www.grimmfairytales.com/en/main

Interactive, narrated, animated versions of several fairy tales plus biographical information, games, and other fun stuff from Kids Fun Canada.

The SurLaLune Fairy-Tale Site

www.surlalunefairytales.com

This personal Web site hosted by a librarian serves as a portal to fairy-tale and folklore studies, featuring forty-four annotated fairy tales, with their histories, cross-cultural tales, and illustrations.

Look for

THE COUNCIL OF MIRRORS,

the ninth book in the series!

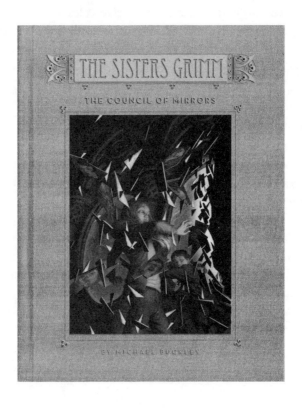

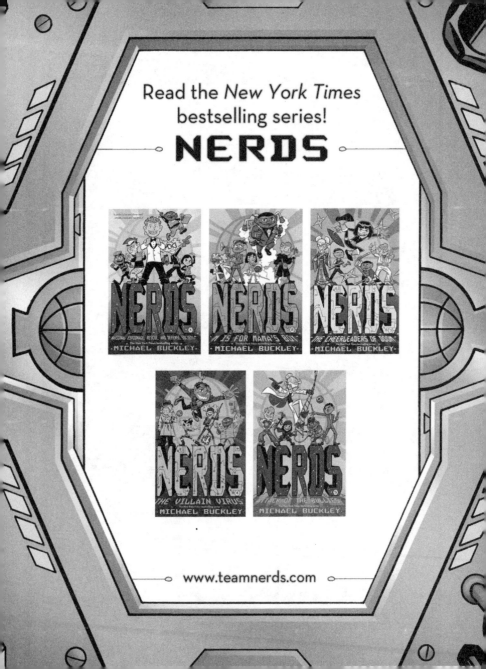